Ron Mueller

Feather-In-The-Wind:

The Eastern Elk Clan

Feather-in-the-Wind: The Eastern Elk Clan

Ron Mueller

Feather-in-Wind

Book 1: The Eastern Elk Clan

Around the World Publishing LLC
4914 Cooper Road Suite 144
Cincinnati, Ohio 45242-9998

ISBN 13: 978-1-68223-226-2
ISBN 10: 1-68223-226-3

The Taelo Series by Ron Mueller
   Taelo: The Early Years
   Taelo: The Golden Feather
   Taelo: The Journey of Discovery
   Taelo: Dangerous Passage
   Taelo: Condor Clan Slingers
   Taelo: Full Circle

Cover Picture By: Hien Mueller
Feather by: KieferPix @ Shutterstock
Cover Design By: Ron Mueller

*To all the women
that have hit the ceiling
and kept on going.*

Ron Mueller

Table of Content

Feather-in-the-Wind: The Eastern Elk Clan

Chapter 1:

As Feather-in-the-Wind sat in a relaxed repose and looked across the lake to the area holding the mounts, she took in the dark green of the forest beyond and the two white capped mountains. It was not yet winter, but she felt the cool evening breeze gently blow her long black hair and cool the back of her neck. She was as relaxed as she could be under the circumstance.

Born a princess in the land of the Condor, she never imagined leaving her homeland. Now she sat looking out at a lake in a northern country that was far from her home.

Her life direction back in her homeland had changed abruptly when she was chosen to become the "Bride" of the Condor. She became the human offering to the Condor King.

Her young life was idyllic and now she realize how privileged she had been.

In a drugged state and totally nude, she had been placed in a cave with all the other princess offerings that went back for at least a hundred years. She would have frozen to death like all the others, but she had been rescued by Quiet Rabbit and Busy Bee, members of the Elk Clan.

She became a member of Taelo's team and journeyed with them through many adventures.

Her courage and bravery and personal skills elevated her stature. She became a valued member of Taelo's team. She faced and survived the giant tiger. Later she barely survived her battle with the giant bear of the North. Her ability to handle animals led her to become both a mount tamer and a leader of the wolves.

Her skill in dealing with people made her respected by those around her. It was more than just respect, people trusted and loved her. Taelo and his team recognized Feather-in-the-Wind: The Eastern Elk Clan.

She had been summed by Wise Owl the leader of the Elk Clan council and had been asked to sit on the bench on which she now reposed. She had not been told why she had been summoned. Her Elk Clan membership was now on its third season.

She thought back to her childhood. She was originally a member of the Condor Clan.

Her father, Star Leaper was the Clan leader. She knew now what a privileged life she had experienced as his daughter.

Her mother, Neiva-of-the-Stream had been one of the best teachers in her life.

And her brother, Bold Walker, her hero in that former life, had been her inspiration. His daring and his gentle coaching style had helped her develop many of the skills that had helped her survive the challenges she had faced.

The evening breeze blew the dry yellow leaves of the willow past her feet. She looked down along the lake to where the willow, now bare of its leaves swayed in the evening breeze. The scene took her back to the cool day when Bold Walker had taught her to ride the Llama.

The memory of the Llama's odor pulled her farther into her reminiscence. She could smell the sweet scent of the damp wool of the Llama.

He had demonstrated how to ride the Llama. He had made it look easy. Bold Walker had picked her up and put her on the Llama's back. He had instructed her to hold on to the neck hair with all her strength. When he let go of her, the Llama took off on a trot that to her was more like a pounding jolt on her behind. Then the Llama abruptly stopped, and she was flipped over its head to the ground.

Once Bold Walker verified that she was alright, he had given her a pat on the behind and chuckled. He made the point that she needed to learn to control the actions of the Llama and not be its victim.

It only took that one time for her to learn. She was in control on every ride after that. She had several more falls as she tried to go faster and faster.

She would have spent all her time riding the many mountain trails, but her mother insisted on her spending time to learn to cook and to make pottery.

Her mother was among the best pottery makers in the Condor Clan. Her glazed pots, mugs and other dishes were prized throughout the village. It took most of a moon cycle to create and finish each item. She painted intricate designs on the white clay surface and then put the item into an oven for drying.

Feather-in-the-Wind was disappointed when on her first pottery making try, half of her items came out of the oven cracked or broken. She was surprised when her mother complemented her on the high number of good items. This taught her that success was not always measured against the high-end potential but against the normally expected result.

The evening moon glimmering on the surface of the lake brought her back to the present and made her look up to where it was rising above the white snow-capped mountains.

The moon made the snow caps shimmer and glow a brilliant white.

She leaned forward and let her hand scratch Bold Walker, the name she had given to her wolf.

She thought of the day her brother pointed to the high-flying Condor that was flying with a bird almost as large.

The second bird was an Eagle.

She remembered him pointing it out because it was a rare sight to have the two giant birds flying in unison.

That was the day that Taelo and his team arrived as had been foretold by the Condor Clan seer.

She went out with Bold Walker and many of the young and adventurous clan members to greet the visitors.

There was a giant among them that appeared to be very different than the rest of them. He was accompanied by a woman of similar appearance.

However, there were two women that caught her eye. To her they displayed an elegance and a confidence that would make anyone take notice.

The approaching group was well dressed and appeared to be friendly.

Their leader came forward followed by a wolf. He greeted her brother and introduced his wolf, Lasher as well.

It was very unusual for a person to have a wolf as a companion.

Then she watched as a second member came forward and introduced himself as Golden Hawk.

He was followed by the two elegant women that she now knew as Quiet Rabbit and Busy Bee. She was immediately struck by their beauty and their self-confidence as they introduced themselves.

There was a third, taller and very talkative woman member of the team that impressed her the constant chatter that often brought out smiles or laughter.

Feather-in-the-Wind later had a laugh was well when she learned that the person's name was Talking Wren. Much later she also began to listen intently because Talking Wren was brilliant.

She recalled the first meeting of the team with her father. He had called together the leadership council. They were gathered around at the base of her father's meeting platform.

She was amazed as Taelo broke all protocol by leading his entire team up the steps of the platform to where her father was seated.

Visitors usually stood at the bottom of the platform to show their respect for the Condor Clan leader.

Taelo greeted her father in the same manner that he had greeted her brother. He put his left hand on her father's right shoulder and then lifted his open right hand, smiled, and introduced himself. Then he introduced each of his team members.

Her father seemed to take the entire event in stride. She was relieved to see his positive reaction. He welcomed them and then led the way to where the welcome dinner was to be served.

It was not clear why Taelo and his team had traveled the great distance to the Condor Mountain Kingdom. She inquired but no one knew.

It also became clear to her that Taelo and his team did not know the purpose of their visit.

She watched curiously as the team split up and seemed to go about and study what the people in the village did each day.

Talking Wren took great interest in the process of making the pottery. She asked what seemed to be an endless number of questions. However, her first oven test impressed her mother and resulted in the least failure that had ever been experienced!

After that, Feather-in-the-Wind paid much closer attention to what Talking Wren said and what she did.

She noted that Taelo and Golden Hawk went about examining how the stone preparers handled the stones to be laid out for a building. They asked almost as many questions as Talking Wren.

She next followed them out to where the Llamas were kept. Again, they asked many questions about the animal, the fur, and the meat.

It was clear to Feather-in-the-Wind that the visitors from the North were keen to learn. They were self-confident and they always thanked those with whom they interacted for having given them their time.

She was impressed by all the team members, and she realized that they were a team that was bound in spirit, and all had common love for learning.

Bold Walker invited Taelo and his team to go to the top of the mountain to visit the Condor nesting area. This was an invitation that was given only to visitors of the highest ranking.

Feather-in-the-Wind immediately asked Bold Walker to let her come along. She not only wanted to see the Condor nest, but she wanted to observe Taelo and his team. They had captured her imagination and she wanted to learn more about them and how they seemed to work together in a seamless ebb and flow of energy.

The climb up the mountain in the thin air was hard on her. She could not imagine how Taelo, and his team felt.

It was clear that Little Otter, the second biggest among Taelo's team struggled on the climb up. Feather-in-the-Wind realized that he was a very shy and quiet person and that his partner was none other than Talking Wren.

This realization caused her to be even more observant of the relationships among the team of visitors.

Busy Bee and Golden Hawk were clearly together. There was no doubt about Burley Bear and Meadow Flower. They were two people that were stronger and more powerful than any human she had ever experienced.

It was the relationship between Quiet Rabbit and Taelo that made her long for a similar relationship for herself. They seemed to exude an energy that empowered the entire team. Neither talked a great deal but when they did it was clear that the rest of the team listened.

On the way to the Condor nesting area, they passed the cave of the Condor Princesses. Entry into the cave was forbidden to all except on the day of the yearly sacrifice of the most desirable virgin. Then two priests would take the next virgin offering as a potential wife to the Condor King and place her next to the last virgin.

She was so enthralled to be going to see the Condor nesting site that it never crossed her mind that she might be the offering to the Condor.

A few sun cycles later, after their return down the mountain Feather-in-the-Wind and her family learned that she had been selected to be the next offering to the Condor King.

She was shocked.

Her mother was in grief.

Her father was outraged because he knew that his adversaries had colluded to make the selection happen.

She learned later that Bold Walker immediately went to his friends from the North to ask for their help.

Before the Wedding Ceremony, Feather-in-the-Wind listened to Bold Walker explain what she needed to. He told her to fake drinking the intoxicating drink the priest would ask her to drink. He told her about a hidden bear skin that would be in the cave and that she was to get into it as soon as the priests had left. He made her repeat his instruction several times.

On the Condor Queen ceremonial day, she was led out to the raised seating area normally reserved for her father. She was displayed and praised for her beauty. She was given the delicious but intoxicating drink. She drank as little as possible but it none the less had its effect. Finally, she was disrobed to show her beauty to the entire Condor Clan.

She was then led up the mountain path to the cave where the Condor Clan placed their offering to the Condor King. She was amazed to see the long line of beautiful young nude women laying as if asleep. The last offering had been a friend of hers and she remembered the one before that.

She faked falling asleep to hasten the departure of the two priests.

Once they had left the cave, she made her way to where the bearskin was hidden. She pulled it out and that was the last she remembered.

When she next awoke, she was warm, and it was clear she was moving.

She sat up to look out from the middle of a travois. The first person she saw was Meadow Flower. Her awakening brought Taelo's team to a standstill. They all came around and greeted her.

Quiet Rabbit and Busy Bee explained how they had entered almost immediately after the two priests left. They had dressed her, put her into the bear skin hide and carried her down the mountain where at the bottom Bold Walker had taken her across the crevasse and placed her on the travois.

They welcomed her to her new life as a member of the Elk Clan and let her know that they were on their way back to the North.

Chapter 2:

On their way the team was met by Tough Hide and a group of his warriors. She watched as Taelo, Burley Bear and Lasher approached Tough Hide. Taelo greeted Tough Hide in the same manner as he had greeted her father.

The team was invited into the Warrior Clan Village.

The Warrior Clan village impressed Feather-in-the-Wind. It was clear to her that the stone masons were masters. Their buildings were massive and rose high overhead.

The team was led to the center of the village to a square where the second leader of the Warrior Clan was introduced. They were also introduced to the rest of people in the square.

Feather-in-the-Wind watched as Taelo stepped forward and offered a gift of friendship to the thirty warriors that his team had faced and defeated on their way South. The gift was an arm band that depicted Taelo's members in their fighting diamond formation surrounded by the thirty warriors. It was a significant gift of friendship by the superior fighters to those they had defeated.

The gifts were accepted by each of the Warrior Clan fighters.

The Warrior Clan co-leader named Sharp Stone, looked at the gift and noted that Taelo's team seemed to have gained another person.

Feather-in-the-Wind was immediately alarmed and frightened. It was clear that Sharp Stone had his eyes on her as he spoke.

The visit was strained, and had it not been for the co-leader named, Tough Hide, Feather-in-the-Wind knew that Sharp Stone would have tried to overpower Taelo's team. It was clear to her that Sharp Stone wanted all the power.

A handful of sun cycles latter, when Taelo decided to leave, Sharp Stone and at least thirty of his fighters surrounded the team. He demanded that Taelo leave her and proceed to the North.

Before she could react, she found herself in the middle of the fighting diamond formation with Quiet Rabbit on her right side and Busy Bee on her left.

They quietly let her know that she was safe.

Feather-in-the-Wind did not feel safe. She watched as Taelo took one step forward as Sharp Stone moved toward him. She wanted to scream to Taelo to watch out. A lick on her hand made her look down at Lasher. He had a deep rumble coming from his throat.

When Sharp Stone drew his knife as he rushed forward, Feather-in-the-Wind watched in amazement as Taelo took a slight smooth unhurried step back, reached back for the handle of his flat blade and swiftly swung it forward.

At the same instant, Lasher leaped in from the side and clamped down on Sharp Stone's wrist that held the knife.

Feather-in-the-Wind had not realized that Lasher had moved from her side.

Taelo's blade cut through Sharp Stone's shoulder and nearly cut him in half. The battle was over in a split moment.

Taelo immediately called for obedience from the supporting Warrior Clan fighters. The Warrior Clan custom bound them to Taelo as their new leader. Taelo in an instant became the co-leader of the Warrior Clan.

At that same moment Tough Hide and his supporters arrived. For a brief moment, Feather-in-the-Wind thought there would be additional fighting, but Taelo offered Tough Hide the loyalty of the fighters that he had just won and the control of the other half of the Warrior Clan that Taelo now controlled. He made it clear that his only desire was to proceed North to his own land.

At that moment, Feather-in-the-Wind knew she would forever follow Taelo.

Their immediate departure resolved all the concerns she had been worrying about.

For the remainder of the journey, she spent as much time as possible learning the fighting skill as a member of the fighting diamond. Quiet Rabbit taught her the use of the sling.

The sling was a weapon that thrilled and inspired her. She practiced for the entire time the team traveled North.

Feather-in-the-Wind was impressed by the greeting given Taelo when the team arrived at the cave of the Others. She knew that this was Burley Bear's and Meadow Flower's clan. The entire Clan of Others cheered their arrival and the Seer of the clan personally greeted Taelo.

The highlight for Feather-in-the-Wind was the warm water pool. She sat in the warm water and looked out at the broad valley beyond. The snow-covered mountains beyond the valley seemed to create the rim of one of her mother's beautifully decorated bowls.

What followed continued to bond Feather-in-the-Wind to the true friends and supporters she had the privilege to be surrounded by.

She missed her family, but she found an inner warmth in the deep bonds she was creating with her adopted clan.

Their stop between the twin white capped mountains next to a small lake was another highlight. With her sling, she had bagged one rabbit for each member of the team. Even Lasher had his own rabbit.

She personally skinned and prepared each rabbit. She took advantage of the guidance and help that she got from Quiet Rabbit, Busy Bee, and Talking Wren. Even though Talking Wren was cooking three very large trout that Taelo, Golden Hawk and Little Otter had caught, she was a continuous advisor on the proper seasoning and cooking of the rabbits.

Then they entered the valley that was to become the home of the Northern Elk Clan. Feather-in-the-Wind would forever remember the waterfall that at the top began as a stream of water and turned into a mist as it settled into the lake at its base. The lake in turn fed the small river that ran along the face of the cliff back to the entrance of the valley.

She knew that Taelo's discovery of a hot water spring and his plans to build the main lodge around it would make this a special place. It would rival the heated pool and the cave of the Others.

The work that followed challenged her, but she felt herself grow both physically and mentally.

The rising of the sun after the night of their arrival was the moment that she awoke and felt the excitement of being a part of a team that was focused on a mission that included building a new home.

The lodge they built was phenomenal. She realized how much Taelo, and his team had learned from her clan. It was also clear that Taelo and Talking Wren extrapolated their learning and took each concept one step farther.

The hot spring was captured and then it was guided in a zig-zag path beneath flat stones to create a heated floor. A stone lined pit was made just outside of the lodge to catch the water leaving the lodge. This Feather-in-the-Wind categorized as a Taelo original.

The lodge roof was made from thin sheets of stone that had been found on the far side of the river. It served the same function as the flat clay sheets on the roofs of the buildings in the Condor Clan village.

The courtyard and the surrounding wall outside of the lodge reminded her of her family's courtyard.

It was clear to her that the gate for the compound, and the massive lodge door made by Burley Bear had to be inspired by the gate they had seen in the entrance to the Warrior Clan village. She complimented him on the marvelous examples of his woodworking skills.

She was with the team when Taelo and Golden Hawk made the discovery of the Cave near the top of the falls. Wall drawings on the cave walls told the history of the Elk Clan. All the Elk Clan members had tears in their eyes as they recounted the stories their parents had told them. They were true stories told to them that were now coming to life.

The moment was one that reminded her of the stories her parents had told her about the Condor Clan. She wondered how many of the stories she had listened to were also true.

It was only a few suns later that she watched Quiet Rabbit hug Taelo as he answered a call from the Ancients to get salt from the salt mine. This was "the" salt mine in the stories of the Elk Clan.

She listened as he let the team know that this was a mission that the ancients had told him to make on his own.

A few sun cycles later as she sat, with both Quiet Rabbit and Busy Bee waiting for the rising of the morning sun, the light from the cave at the top of the falls began blinking a message. It was Taelo letting them know that an enemy threatened and that he was going to eliminate the threat.

She volunteered to with Golden Hawk, who planned to go to the cave to help. Golden Hawk rejected her offer since he did not know what the situation was that he would face.

Two anxiety dominated sun cycles later, the light from the top of cliff once again flashed. It let the team know that Taelo and Golden Hawk would be bringing more than twenty rescued people to the lodge.

The team went into action. She went out and bagged at least a dozen rabbits that she and Talking Wren used to create a stew to feed the large group of people that they were sure would arrive and need to eat.

The group of people looked starved and emaciated. Feather-in-the-Wind watched as Quiet Rabbit limited the amount of food that each person ate. She learned that a person that has not eaten well for a long time will get sick if they eat too much too soon.

She also learned about someone who would later be very special for her.

A young man, Running Stag, received praise from both Taelo and Golden Hawk for his bravery. He had been the single person to support Taelo in the battle against the cannibals and he had helped rescue Golden Hawk from a group holding him hostage.

Feather-in-the-Wind remembered thinking that Running Stag was barely as tall and no larger than herself. We are both small and brave she thought.

That event was quickly followed by Taelo, Golden Hawk, Burley Bear and Little Otter going out to the rescue of another group of people.

Taelo and his wolf pulled sled returned first with a group of children and a mother and her infant.

She then watched as he recruited Running Stag to return with him to rescue another load of people.

Burley Bear, Little Otter and Golden Hawk returned just as the storm that had threatened them all day hit. It was a fierce storm and its arrival made visibility impossible. Everyone huddled in the warmth of the lodge.

The yelping and howling of the wolves signaled the arrival of the fourth sled. Running Stag was the person that was guiding the wolf team, but he credited Lasher with getting them through the blinding snow. He accented his point by stating that his sled had come in through the gate and almost hit the lodge.

She watched in amazement as Lasher signaled his desire to go out into the storm by clamping Running Stag's wrist in his mouth and dragging him to the lodge door.

Even Quiet Rabbit commented that she had never seen Lasher accept anyone as he had accepted Running Stag. She got a hide to wrap around Lashers body and made sure that his feet had dry booties.

Then Running Stag opened the door and Lasher bolted out into the driving snow.

Later, Lasher returned with Taelo. He had gone through the storm to find Taelo and then had led Taelo and a group of twenty back to the lodge.

Taelo was already her hero. He was a hero to his team. Now he was a hero to more than ninety new people.

He was the first to call all of them the Northern Elk Clan.

She took a new look at the slender young man named Running Stag.

The moons that followed saw the new clan blend and coalesce.

She spent her time teaching pottery making and the use of the sling. She also participated in Golden Hawk's language lessons and in Quiet Rabbit's and Meadow Flower's cooking lessons.

Talking Wren became a logics coach and pointed out how the village around the mound on which the lodge was built should be developed.

Feather-in-the-Wind absorbed and grew from the coaching she received from all her supporters.

The "Northern Elk Clan" unanimously agreed with Taelo to arrive to the Elk Clan's meeting early . They followed Taelo's plan to set up the camp sites and greet each Elk Clan with an arrival meal.

She listened, observed, and learned from all her mentors on how to influence and manage the change that they were bringing to the rest of the Elk Clan.

She was expecting to be a member of the Northern Elk Clan that she was sure would be led by Taelo.

She was surprised at the dozens of proposals she received to become someone's mate. She asked if this was always the case when the Elk Clan gathered? Quiet Rabbit, Busy Bee and Talking Wren laughed and told her that all the beautiful women had to fight suiters off. They claimed that because of their looks, they on the other had run their mates down.

She had no interest in any of the proposals. She wanted to be free from such commitment.

The evening when the Elk Clan council agreed to another sub-clan, the Northern Elk was established. She was shocked when she learned that Wise Owl had named White Swan, Taelo's mother as the first woman to lead an Elk Clan.

A woman had been named as the new Leader of the Northern Elk Clan.

Chapter 3:

The journey back to the Northern Elk Clan Village was a blur. Feather-in-the-Wind had been in a state of shock.

How was it that Taelo was overlooked?

She noticed that Taelo and Golden Hawk were both missing.

Were they disappointed too?

She asked Running Stag what he thought and was surprised when he simply said that it had been Taelo that had pushed to have his mother named clan leader.

She should have known better than to have had such a concern. She soon heard about and immediately asked Quiet Rabbit to let her be part of a new venture that Taelo planned to lead to the East.

She was surprised to hear that Taelo had already accepted a request from Running Stag. She was pleased when she too was accepted.

She learned that in addition to herself, Saber Scar and his mate Meadow Flower would also be part of the team.

The journey to the East was to begin while winter still ruled. But before departing they stopped at the cave of the Clan of Others. There she once again enjoyed the hot pool. This was the time that she learned that Quiet Rabbit had been the person that had stitched closed the saber claw marks that resulted in the name change from Rolling Stone to Saber Scar.

Meadow Flower now his mate claimed that Rolling Stone had seemed a little boring to her but with the name Saber Scar he had a new aura of power.

The team left after Taelo had received the visions and guidance of Broken Spear the seer of the Others.

The winter cold was barely bearable for her. She was always looking for one more hide layer to put on.

She took up running with the wolves pulling the sleds to keep warm. She was surprised when Running Stag joined and kept her company.

It was the hunt of the buffaloes in preparation to their arrival to the Eastern Elk Clan where she learned how to guide an entire herd of buffalo.

At the suggestion of Quiet Rabbit and Busy Bee she had taken off her heavy coat and most of her other clothing items. She went out in her simple one layer of clothing. She was surprised that she kept warm during the run with the buffalo.

However, when she was done and totally covered by wet mud, snow, and the foul-smelling buffalo dung, she immediately thought she would freeze, and she put on her coat over her dirty body. She figured it was better to have a dirty coat and survive.

She watched as Running Stag seemed to have the same reaction as she had.

He was slowly becoming a more important figure in her thinking. They both helped in preparing for their arrival at the Grazing Elk Clan village.

The arrival to the village was well orchestrated. The team guided their wolf pulled, heavily meat loaded sleds in a circle around the village.

She was pleased with the reception they got. It was clear to her that Taelo was held in high esteem. Bringing the Grazing Elk Clan, a gift of three buffalo, also made a huge difference in their reception.

The team planned to leave their sled wolves with the Grazing Elk Clan. Taelo, Golden Hawk and Saber Scar identified the sled wolf keepers.

While they trained the sled wolf keepers, she taught the use of the sling.

The sling was so popular that she spent all her sunlight hours teaching the boys, girls and about half the women.

When Taelo, over an evening dinner, announced that he was ready to move on, she and the rest of the team readily agreed.

Lily, one of the women who had been rescued from the cannibals by Taelo joined the team. She had come to the Grazing Elk Clan with three other women rescued from the cannibals, but she was the only one that had not found a mate.

It was clear to Feather-in-the-Wind that Lily and Running Stag were very close. Their common horrible experience had bonded them for life.

As they left, she waved goodbye to all her new friends and then joyfully jogged to the front where Taelo and Golden Hawk were talking about the mountains ahead.

The team crossed the mountains and came down into a vast plain.

She was among the first to see the new four-legged animal. Little did she know just how this newly discovered animal would change her life and that of the rest of the team.

The team spent most of the sun cycle in discussion and suggesting a name for this new animal.

She was impressed when Quiet Rabbit scratched all the suggested names into the dirt. Quiet Rabbit then gave each person four stones. The person was to pick their favorite names and put the stones below the name. The four stones could be put down on one name or they could be spread out.

Taelo was very elegant in describing how the animal would be used by the team.

He was the person that suggested the name Mount.

Feather-in-the-Wind put her four stones down below the Mount name. She hugged Running Stag when he did the same. Then it was Saber Scar's turn for a hug. Lily smiled and put her four on the same name.

Taelo smiled as he put down one stone.

He put one each under names suggested by her, Running Stag and Saber Scar.

Quiet Rabbit put one down under Mount but put one stone on three other names.

It only took a few more stones and the pile of stones under the Mount name was clearly the winning pile.

When she asked why Taelo had not put all his stones on the name he had suggested, he replied that his stones were unnecessary and other names deserved recognition.

The next sun cycle two scout teams were sent out to find a good campsite where they could train the new animal that they had named the Mount. She and Running Stag, one of the scout teams, discovered the waterfall and the area they ended up calling Paradise.

A wide thin sheet of water fell some thirty feet to a clear translucent blue green pool. The bottom was clearly visible and when they jumped in, they discovered it was much deeper than their eyes and mind understood. As astonishing, fish the size of her arm were visible and so numerous they seemed to be a small buffalo herd grazing the bottom.

The water was so cold that they almost immediately got out on a slightly sloped flat stone ledge where they had chosen to make their camp.

On the other side, to the right side of the falls was a wide meadow threatening to go green but currently graced with a variety of dried stems of wildflowers. The meadow seemed to be just the right size to hold and graze the new animal they planned to capture.

This was the first time the two of them spent a night keeping each other warm.

As the sun crested the horizon, she and Running Stag jogged back to the team They were surprised that the team had crossed over to their side of the river. They later learned of the failure of Quiet Rabbit and Busy Bee to find a suitable camp.

The two of them excitedly described Paradise. They declared that they found the perfect place to house and train the mounts they planned to capture.

When the team came within sight of the falls, Taelo and the rest of the team readily agreed with the name they had given to this location. They all agreed that it was indeed Paradise.

Feather-in-the-Wind knew that she and Running Stag were being treated as equals to the other team members when Taelo asked the two to find the herd of mounts that the team had seen earlier and mark a trail back to them.

His plan to capture one mount for each of them and some additional mounts to carry their personal gear excited her.

She and Running Stag eagerly set out on their mission. When they located the mount herd, they spent time to examine them and to decide on which one they might want.

They found the perfect one for Saber Scar. It had a similar scar on its chest that was almost a match to the scar he had on his chest.

They spotted a mother mount and a younger horse that seemed it to her, should be hers. Feather-in-the-Wind wanted the young horse and stated that the mother would probably be perfect for Lily.

Running Stag declared that any of the mounts would do.

He spotted one mount that was much larger than the rest that he thought should be Taelo's.

As they returned to camp, they built stone piles to hold up long poles with a black feather tied on top. They placed the piles as far apart as possible. The feather at the top of the pole was always visible from the next pile.

They returned late in the evening below a thick plane of black clouds. They knew they were just ahead of a threatening storm.

The smell of roasting meat had their mouths watering long before they saw the fire.

The storm that arrived that evening dumped enough snow that everything was buried beneath almost half a spear depth.

It took the team almost to the sun's zenith to dig out and organize themselves.

Taelo declared that they would make their way to where the mounts were located and decide whether to capture them when they got there.

She and Running Stag basked in the praise they got for having put up such a good set of markers.

The long valley where the mounts were located must have been wind-blown. The grasses were snow covered but clearly visible.

She and Running Stag pointed out the mounts that they had previously identified.

She was pleased that Saber Scar immediately agreed that the mount with the scar on its chest was perfect for him.

He suggested that the one with the scar on its back would be perfect for Running Stag.

This caught Feather-in-the-Wind by surprise. It was then she learned how Running Stag had been wounded as he fought and killed two powerful cannibal warriors. The scar had been sewn up by Quiet Rabbit who now commented that her two patients, Running Stag and Saber Scar, had both demonstrated grit and silently let her sew them up.

The mounts were captured, and Feather-in-the-Wind discovered that the songs her mother sang to her as a child seemed to calm the mounts.

Soon the team members were all singing gently as they led a mount back to the camp. Marigold suggested that Saber Scar get someone else to sing to his mount.

Feather-in-the-Wind's experience in learning to ride the Llama gave her some insight on how to ride the mount. However, Taelo had the experience in how to tame the buffalo.

He engaged her in discussing how the mount might be trained and they agreed that first the mount would learn to accept carrying the load of a log on each side of its body. Taelo strapped two logs together in such a fashion that the straps went across the mount's back.

Once the mount accepted being led around with the two logs. It was time to have each mount carry a person.

Feather- in- the-wind volunteered to be the first person to ride each mount. She lost count in the number of times she was thrown off a jumping mount. She was thankful that each time either Taelo, Golden Hawk or Saber Scar caught her and broke her fall.

After she successfully rode a mount, its owner was next to ride it.

The owner normally had the experience of the mount wanting to throw them off. This Taelo commented was because the owner was heavier than Feather-in-the-Wind and the mount did not recognize their smell.

The exception had been Mother, Lily's mount. Lily had fed her each morning and had brought a treat that she fed her before getting on. She also sang a lullaby as she fed her. When Lilly got on, Mother looked back at her, shook her head, and proceeded to trot in the circle made by all the team members.

Once the mounts were trained, Taelo declared it was time to travel.

Feather-in-the-Wind was ready to move on. She was in tip-top shape from having been the main mount tamer. Now she was ready to ride her mount and relax.

Each day she got better at riding her mount. She could stand on its back and keep up with the rest of the team. She could mount and dismount while on the go. It seemed to her that she and her mount Star Leaper, named after her father, were synchronized, and anticipated each-other's movements.

She was in love with her mount. She liked all of them and talked to them all. She laughed when Running Stag stepped in front of the next mount and volunteered to talk to her.

The next valley they came to, appeared to be a sea of mastodon and buffalo moving slowly as they grazed. It was the valley they needed to cross but it was obvious that the team would not be able to do that during the present sun cycle.

She joined the rest of the team in setting up camp next to the small stream they had just crossed.

She mentioned that she was going out with her sling to get some rabbits or other small game for their dinner.

She went out on foot but was joined by Saber Scar and Running Stag who had chosen to ride their mounts.

She was listening to Saber Scar complain about that fact that she had bagged all the small game when the eyes she looked into ahead of her made her raise her hand and quietly tell everyone to slowly back up.

Then the giant tiger leaped out of the forest and ran straight at her. In a reflex action, she dropped her sling, pulled out her skinning blade and ran directly at the beast. At the last instant, she went into a slide and with both hands and all her might she drove her blade into the tiger's chest. She continued to slide and rolled out behind the tiger. She got to her feet. She had no weapon. She expected to die but she would die fighting.

With spear in hand, Saber Scar jumped off his mount and shouted at the tiger. Running Stag was shooting arrow after arrow into the side and shoulder of the tiger.

The tiger charged Saber Scar, knocked the spear aside and was about to leap on top of him.

Feather-in-the-Wind reacted instinctively. The tiger was about to kill Saber Scar. Shouting at the top of her voice, she ran toward the beast and with all her might she launched herself like a spear into the side of the beast.

She heard her shoulder and bones in her ribs cracking but she was exhilarated by the fact that the beast's jaws and claws had missed Saber Scar.

She had continued to push with all her might.

Just before the world went dark, she saw Saber Scar using her blade to repeatedly stab the tiger from below and watched Running Stag drive a spear down the tiger's throat.

The scream of the Eagle accompanied her journey into the dark.

She opened her eyes as Taelo. Quiet Rabbit, Golden Hawk and Busy Bee arrived.

She was so concerned about Saber Scar, who was bleeding from four deep slashes across his chest that she got up claiming to be alright. The pain she felt put her on the verge of fainting and she stumbled forward to kneel at his side.

Quiet Rabbit pushed her gently aside.

Feather-in-the-Wind made no objections when Golden Hawk lifted her up to Busy Bee to go back to the camp.

The last thing she heard was Saber Scar thanking her for saving his life.

"He has it backwards," she mumbled.

The pain was much worse on the subsequent sun cycles. Taelo and the team camped for almost a moon cycle while she and Saber Scar recovered.

She still experienced some pain as they finally continued their journey toward the East. She again gave thanks for her mount. She did not think that she would have been able to keep up with the team if they were jogging.

The long-delayed trip across the valley was uneventful except for a pack of wolves that shadowed them all the way until they came to the mighty river.

She watched as Taelo walked out with pieces of buffalo meat that he fed to the wolves. He thanked them for providing protection from any tigers and advised them to enjoy the meal and then go on their way.

It seemed to Feather-in-the-Wind that the wolves understood because they left as Taelo had requested.

Chapter 4:

The river was that widest that Feather-in-the-Wind had ever seen. She remembered her brother, Bold Walker describing a river he had traveled on that he could not see across. She could see across this one but wondered how the team would get all their supplies across.

She watched as Taelo walked upstream and repeatedly threw a stick out to measure how fast the water was flowing. Then, once he had decided where the crossing would start, he and Golden Hawk swam out to an island that was about a third of the way across.

The two swam back and Taelo explained how they would cross and set the team to work to assemble rafts on which to float their belongings and themselves.

Taelo led his mount out into the water to test its ability to swim. He was pleased to learn that the mount seemed to enjoy the water and swam well.

They crossed the mighty river in two steps. The first was to cross to the island. That went smoothly. Then a fierce rainstorm arrived, and the river immediately began to rise.

Taelo immediately sent the team across.

The river current became powerful, the wind-blown rain was blinding, and the current caused the rafts to shoot down stream faster than a thrown spear.

She almost lost her mount. Ironically, it was her mount that by its natural instincts was able to get out of the water and pull her to safety as she held on to its tail.

She cared for her mount first and rewarded it immediately with a treat. She followed the rest of the team through the rain to a huge hollow tree that Taelo had found. The rain continued for the next two sun cycles.

The territory they were in was forest covered, rich in berries and populated by an abundance of wildflowers. Feather-in-the-Wind wandered the terrain and was usually accompanied by Running Stag.

Taelo had made a point of reminding the team that they should not go out by themselves.

She would forever remember the fateful morning she took Lasher with her for an early morning walk. The sun was threatening the horizon and she was the only one awake. She and the team had all been cooped up inside the hollow of the giant tree.

She wandered aimlessly uphill to an open area that was bordered on the far side by what seemed to be berry bushes of some type. As she went toward it to investigate, a giant bear, the biggest she had ever seen, stood up in the middle of the open area and began sniffing the air. It must have gotten her scent.

She immediately started to back away. When the bear advanced in her direction she turned and ran and climbed up the nearest tree.

Lasher distracted the bear and gave her just enough time to get up out of the bear's reach.

The bear stood at its full height and leaned against the tree. He was trying to break it! It seemed that he might succeed. On one of the sways, Feather-in-the-Wind was able to jump to a close by, larger pine and climb farther up.

Lasher was still growling and trying to distract the bear but to no avail. The bear was ignoring the wolf and had its eyes on a more desirable treat.

She instructed Lasher to find Taelo. When she mentioned Taelo's name Lasher immediately turned and left the open meadow toward where the camp was located.

Most bears can climb trees and pursue their prey but this one was so large that it could not climb straight up the pine she had settled in.

She watched as it sat at the base growling, grunting, and looking up at her.

Taelo and the rest of team arrived a short time later.

She watched as Taelo began talking to the bear. He suggested the bear leave or otherwise he might meet its doom.

An eagle let out a loud cry at the same time as the bear charged towards Taelo. Taelo lifted his arms into the air and let out a huge roar. The bear stopped, stood, and did the same. Then is lumbered forward.

Taelo was within reach of the bear.

From her height up in the tree, it appeared that Taelo was a very small person, and the bear was impossibly huge.

Feather-in-the-Wind watched as Taelo stepped in toward the bear! He drove his spear upward with all his might as the bear seemed to hug him.

She was on her way down from the tree as the bear slowly fell forward toward Taelo. She jumped down and ran to where Taelo was trapped below the giant bear. He had succeeded in killing it, but he was trapped under it.

Once the bear was rolled off Taelo, Quiet Rabbit examined the four puncture wounds in Taelo's back.

Feather-in-the-Wind was shocked when Taelo, after checking to make sure she was safe, passed out.

She spent the next seven sun cycles both during the day and during the night quietly talking to and caring for Taelo.

She blamed herself for what had happened to him.

Later, when she apologized for getting him injured, he jokingly asked if she had called the bear?

When she responded that she of course had not called the bear, he went on to ask if she had made the bear attack him?

She responded that she would never have done such a thing.

He smiled at her and made the point that there was nothing to apologize about.

Almost immediately after his recovery, Taelo had the team moving east. He was still recovering from his puncture wounds and often seemed to sleep as they rode.

Feather-in-the-Wind took to riding her mount just behind him to be there in case he fell off. She laughed when Taelo looked back to her and assured her that he would not fall off even if he actually did fall asleep.

A few sun cycles later, Feather-in-the-Wind almost rode into the path of a monstrous, dangerous looking beast. She backed her mount and loaded her sling. She thought her sling would be useless if the giant attacked. It was as large or larger than a buffalo and had claws as long as her arm.

The giant ignored all of them as it pulled a limb down and stripped the leaves off. It quickly became clear that it was a plant eater. It and a companion beast slowly made their way through the forest stopping periodically to pull down tree limps and eat the leaves.

While they were watching the giant plant eaters, a pride of lions had approached them from behind. Lily spotted them and immediately sounded the alarm as she began using her sling.

Feather-in-the-Wind joined Quiet Rabbit, Busy Bee, and Lily and together the barrage of stone from their slings drove the lions off.

Taelo suggested they ride on and get out of the lion's territory.

She once again rode point as they headed toward the East.

She was surprised when one sun cycle later Taelo seemed to wander off. She could not tell what he was doing but she, like the rest of the team, followed him.

Taelo followed a honeybee to a huge tree where the bee's nest was located! How he had managed to follow it was a question the team talked about.

Feather-in-the-Wind watched as Taelo climbed up the tree to examine the honeybee's nest.

She was surprised that the bees did not attack him. He moved slowly as he closely examined the entry to the hive. When he came down, he gave instructions to Running Stag on where to cut a hole into the trunk of the tree and how big the opening should be. Running Stag was to carefully cut a square that could later be put back.

Feather in the Wind went up with Running Stag to cut the opening. She practiced staying calm as the bees flew around.

She relaxed and enjoyed the view from her lofty height. It took Running Stag a good part of the afternoon sun cycle to accomplish carving the opening. She had climbed down and helped in preparing the bags the honey would be put into.

Taelo went up and carefully remove the honeycombs and put them into the leather bags that she and Lilly had prepared for each team member.

When she was handed her filled bag, she quickly tasted the sweat golden nectar. It was a heavenly treat.

Taelo instructed Running Stag in how to put the wood back to close the opening.

She asked why Taelo was so thorough to have sealed the edges of the opening with bee's wax? He smiled and replied that he had taken the honey from the bees, but he did not want their home to be damaged and that someday someone else might want more honey.

The team enjoyed a sumptuous dinner of bear meat roasted over the fire as it was basted with honey on each turn of the spit. Roasted onions and the clear water from the small stream rounded out one of the best meals that Feather-in-the-Wind had enjoyed.

She mentioned that the meal was a great way to celebrate Taelo's complete recovery. Golden Hawk picked up on this and commented that perhaps Taelo had physically recovered but he was not sure about complete recovery. Saber Scar added that Taelo seemed to sleep more and run less.

Taelo joined the banter by claiming to have new powers of observation and there were only a few members still in good standing.

Lily for her cooking ability.

Feather-in-the-Wind for her thoughtfulness.

And Quiet Rabbit for holding his hand and squeezing it.

He held out his left hand that Quiet Rabbit was holding.

Everyone had another bite to eat, and the banter continued.

After the sun went down and the stars began twinkling overhead Feather-in-the-Wind crawled into the comfort of her sleeping hide and was immediately asleep.

Chapter 5:

The mountains slowly came into view and dominated the sky ahead of the team. They were not as high as those they had left behind, but Feather-in-the-Wind saw that they still displayed the white of snow at the top but, they were covered by trees and a smattering of flowers almost to their peeks. She wondered if there was a way through that would allow the team to travel with their mounts and to pull their travois behind their pack mounts.

She was sitting on her mount absorbing the grand beauty of the skyline ahead when Taelo called a halt and asked everyone to gather around. He announced that the team would camp by the creek they had been following upstream. He went on to say that the team needed to find a path that would take them through the mountains.

He asked Quiet Rabbit, Busy Bee, and Golden Hawk to each select a partner and go out and see if they could find a path through the mountains that would allow the team and their mounts to get through.

Feather-in-the-Wind was thrilled when Quiet Rabbit selected her as a partner. She watched Running Stag's positive reaction when Busy Bee selected him. Golden Hawk pointed to Saber Scar who nodded in agreement.

She, Quiet Rabbit, and her wolf Bold Walker set out toward the north. Busy Bee, Running Stag and his wolf Arrow would be the team in the middle and Golden Hawk and Saber Scar would be the team on the southern flank.

She and Bold Walker were out front setting the pace. Quiet Rabbit periodically called for a stop. She would point out the features that were ahead of them and suggest adjustments to the direction they were going.

Though she knew that both of them had never been in the area before, it seemed to Feather-in-the-Wind that Quiet Rabbit knew where she was going.

Then ahead Feather-in-the-Wind saw a stream flowing between two peaks.

She and Walker ran ahead and down into a small valley that sat at the foot of a passage between the mountains. The clear water of the stream tumbled energetically down a long rocky stream bed. The stream went as far as she could see then it took a bend and disappeared.

46

Quiet Rabbit suggested the two travel as far as the bend in the stream. She also suggested that both of them keep an eye out for fish that they could have for their dinner.

Feather-in-the-Wind killed two rabbits for Bold Walker with her sling. She then concentrated on finding her meal and soon had speared a large trout for herself.

She had watched as Quiet Rabbit had skillfully speared three similar sized trout. She knew that all three of them would eat well that evening.

The water in the stream was cold but refreshing as she dipped herself into a pool that was almost a half spear deep. She and Quiet Rabbit had both eaten and were bathing before crawling into their sleeping hides.

As they stood by the fire drying off, she admired Quiet Rabbits full form. Her own shape was more like the flat sheets of rock sliding down toward the stream. She also saw that she was almost a head shorter. Well, there was nothing to do but to blame her mother. Thoughts of her family brought a surge of warm nostalgia and a grey sadness.

After a sound sleep and before the sun was up to warm the air, Quiet Rabbit was leading the way back down stream.

Feather-in-the-Wind was ready to eat. Several rabbits met their fate, but it was a fat ground hog that caused them to stop and take the time to light a fire and prepare a combination, rabbit, ground hog and fish early morning meal.

They were at the point where the small river or maybe they should call it a large stream ran into a long valley before meeting the foothills beyond.

The two of them chatted about the beauty of the surroundings and the good taste of salted roast ground hog. They both watched as Walker scared a rabbit and tried to run it down. It was a relief when he came back and chewed on the bones of the ground hog.

As the sun slowly descended toward the far horizon, they saw the thin white smoke of the campfire.

From past experience this was the way that Taelo always made the camp's location visible.

They were the last to return but they were ones that had the best news.

Feather-in-the-Wind was pleased when Quiet Rabbit gave her the credit of finding the stream and what seemed to be a good way through the mountains. Quiet Rabbit ask her to describe the location and what she thought about the way.

This, Feather-in-the-Wind knew positioned her as an equal. It was an honor that Quiet Rabbit was bestowing on her.

She stood and slowly spoke slowly and clearly trying to sound as much like Broken Spear as possible. She described the beauty and how rich the game and fish seemed to be. After the description, she walked over to Quiet Rabbit and gave her a hug and whispered a thank-you.

Early the next sun cycle, she led the team toward the chosen passage through the mountains.

48

Running Stag rode beside her and congratulated her on her elevation as an equal with the older members of the team.

The team enjoyed an easy passage through the mountains. A few sun cycles later she was riding her mount at the rear of the team when the white gulls that always flew close to the sea were spotted.

She moved her mount toward the front to listen to Taelo's instructions to the team.

She eagerly trotted her mount out ahead. She was looking forward to reaching the sea.

The team arrived at a random location, and it was the eagle in the sky that verified to the team that the small cove with a cliff on one side and an island on the other side was the location where they were supposed to be.

Feather-in-the-Wind jumped down from her mount and ran to the water.

It was cold.

The waves were small because the narrow stone cliff jutting into the sea on one side and the island on the other that formed the cove, blocked the force of the larger waves that could be seen farther out beyond the cove opening.

Taelo rode along the cliff to a windblown, huge trunked ancient tree. Its branches created a large, shaded area over ground that was a mix of sand, grasses, and small shrubs.

Feather-in-the-Wind waited patiently as each pair on the team picked the spot they desired, then she looked around and selected her area next to a bush at the edge of the large tree's longest limb. This spot would give her the morning sun, the late afternoon shade and if she needed, she could tie a line between the bush and the tree limb to make an overhead cover.

Later she enjoyed the meal of the large fish speared by Quiet Rabbit and grilled by Lily. She had contributed a few clams that were put at the edge of the fire and Golden Hawk had harvested some seaweed that put a finishing touch to the meal.

Afterwards she took a quick bath in the cold sea and returned to crawl into her sleeping hide. She cast her eyes to the heavens and took in all the lights from those that had gone before her. Sleep came soon after and she spent an easy restful night.

After a light meal of some elk meat prepared by Lilly. She and Running Stag rode their mounts down the coast. She noted that Saber Scar was riding his mount a distance behind them. She knew that he was doing so for her protection.

The sun had just passed the zenith when an eagle cried overhead. She and Running Stag looked at each other and in unison turned their mounts back toward their camp. Feather-in-the-Wind took note at the speed that Saber Scar was making on his large mount. He would get back to the cove first.

The size of the shark that Taelo, Golden Hawk and Lily were pulling onto the beach when they arrived was the largest that any of the team had ever experienced.

Saber Scar dismounted and proceeded to smash the shark's skull with his war hammer. He then tied a rope to the tail of the shark and used his mount to pull the shark all the way out of the water.

As she rode in, Feather-in-the-Wind watched as Quiet Rabbit and Busy Bee swam to shore and ran to Taelo and Golden Hawk. She listened as Busy Bee still in tears hugged Golden Hawk and asked him if he was alright. It seemed that Busy Bee who was exploring the island with Quiet Rabbit and Marigold had seen the size of the attacking shark and was sure Golden Hawk would die.

Golden Hawk recounted his experience and thanked Taelo for being able to fly. It took careful listening by Feather-in-the-Wind for her to understand that Taelo had jumped from the cliff with his spear, to save Golden Hawk.

She estimated the distance and she agreed with Golden Hawk that Taelo could fly.

Running Stag measured the shark with his spear. It was three and one-half spears long and a full half spear at its widest. It was an understatement to say it was huge.

She listened to Taelo describe how Lily's shouting had brought him out of his sleep. And then he saw the shark bearing down on Golden Hawk. He likened it to seeing a full-grown mountain pine attacking a squirrel. Golden Hawk looked like a small morsel for the giant fish.

She decided to stay out of the way as the team concentrated on skinning and processing the shark. She walked the beach and collected clams and caught several large lobster that she brought to Lily. She then helped to prepare the evening meal.

The shark was the big event at the cove. The rest of the time was spent in the salting and drying of the shark meat and the scraping and preparation of the hide. Feather-in-the-Wind was happy to learn how to do both.

She watched as Taelo, and Golden Hawk spent time walking the beach and talking. It seemed to her that they were recuperating from their unforgettable experience.

Then Taelo announced to the team that it was time to move toward the South. He estimated that it was now the long hunt period for the Elk Clan. This season they would miss the clan gathering.

He shared the surprise he had arranged for the Northern Elk Clan and for his mother, White Swan.

He had arranged with Burley Bear to light a fire that would send white smoke into the air. This had been what Taelo, and Golden Hawk had done several seasons ago to signal that the Elk Hide Clan had a way to camp by the lakeside. It had been the first time the two had been given a team to lead.

In what had become a practiced habit, the team packed and cleaned their camp area. Little trace of their presence could be seen and, in a few sun cycles the area would appear to never have been visited.

The team had traveled a short distance down the coast when the sand under her mount's feet began to sing!

Feather-in-the-Wind jumped down and ran through the sand. It was magical! She could make the sand sing the simple tunes her mother had hummed to her when she was a young girl!

The entire team took time to play in this magical sand.

Quite Rabbit and Busy Bee coordinated and sang a simple lullaby to the tune they made with the sand.

Saber Scar and Marigold stomped out a rhythm to a chant the Others often used.

Taelo recognized it and commented that it had been the chant that the Others had used during the processing of the whale.

The entire team laughed as the three wolves growled and howled and frolicked up and down the beach.

Finally, Taelo pointed to an eagle flying toward the mountains and said it was time to move on.

The team left the beach in laughter and talking about how much fun that bricf time had been.

They named the beach, Singing Sand Beach. It would be a story they would all talk about for a longtime.

Chapter 6:

Feather-in-the-Wind was soon riding her mount through a thick towering forest. The canopy overhead seemed to be an interlocked series of branches trying to keep the sunlight at bay. The maple and oak trees seemed to have joined together as partners. She observed that that the curious squirrels had no problem following the team as it rode through at a leisurely pace.

Thinking of the zenith meal, Feather-in-the-Wind suggested that they bag a few of the fatter ones. Soon after, she and the rest of the team had a sufficient quantity to stop, build a small cooking fire and enjoy a roast squirrel feast.

It was a good decision later when the sun was threatening the far horizon the solid canopy gave way to a more open forest sprinkled with a series of small clearings. A small stream running through one small clearing made a good point to stop.

Feather-in-the-Wind accompanied by Running Stag, walked the stream, and gathered a sack full of large crabs. They returned with their dinner contribution and found that Quiet Rabbit and Busy Bee had constructed Taelo's now famous fish trap that had yielded a trout for each team member. As always, the team ate well.

For more than half a moon cycle, Feather-in-the-Wind and the team enjoyed good weather and made similar evening stops. Marigold commented that she was worried that this calm and wonderful time might be the calm before a storm.

It was the next sun cycle when Saber Scar warned that on his circular scouting ride, he had spotted a pack of wolves following the team.

Feather-in-the-Wind took note that Saber Scar commented that the size of the wolf tracks made them at least as large as dire wolves. She now understood the reason for the low throaty growls coming from Walker, Arrow and Lasher.

Taelo suggested they find a good defendable campsite.

She, Running Stag and Golden Hawk rode ahead of the team seeking such a camp. The three were accompanied by Walker and Arrow.

Not far ahead they came to a shallow river with a small island. The rocky island was heavily covered by willows and other small trees. An abundance of small boulders made it an ideal place to set up a defensive camp.

She and Golden Hawk began gathering willow poles. They were counting on Walker and Arrow to warn them of any wolves. Running Stag had ridden back to guide the team.

Taelo arrived and asked that she and Lily tether the mounts in the center of what he was planning to make into a defendable compound.

She listened as Taelo gave each team member an assignment. He, Marigold and Saber Scar had the task of gathering and placing small boulders in a circle. The boulders would act as anchors for the base of the pole stockade he had the team building.

She and Lily tended the mounts and made fire pits just inside of the perimeter created by the boulders. They also spaced the poles and got them ready to be bound together.

She helped Busy Bee and Quiet Rabbit when they began to construct the perimeter fence. She and Lily wove the rope around the bottom while Quiet Rabbit and Busy Bee wove the rope in the middle. After bringing in the last load of poles, Golden Hawk and Running Stag joined them in getting the rope on the perimeter poles. The poles were space about a hand width apart.

She watched as Saber Scar and Marigold rode their mounts and led the four load mounts as they went out to gather firewood. They wanted to gather enough dry wood to keep all the perimeter fires burning through the night.

Taelo and Golden Hawk began standing the stockade up. They tied the thinner willow sticks to the stockade's top edge. This stiffened and gave the barrier some strength. From the inside, every half spear length they drove a stake into the ground and angled a strong pole from the stake to the middle of the perimeter wall to hold it up.

As the perimeter took shape, Feather-in-the-Wind began to relax. Taelo was driving the team hard, but they would have a very defendable structure around them.

When the bottom rope had gone full circle, she and Running Stag began to pound in the stakes to be used to hold up the perimeter.

She watched as Taelo, and Golden Hawk created a gate that could be opened and easily closed. He thanked them for pounding in the stakes and asked them to tie each pole securely to the perimeter. The poles provided the wall the strength to keep it from collapsing.

The dark grey almost black clouds and the distant lightening warned the team of an approaching storm and a rainy night.

Poles were used to hold up hide covers to provide protection from the rain. The individual sleeping areas were placed on a layer of poles to keep them dry.

Lily organized the cooking area. She put up a cover to protect it from the anticipated rain.

Feather-in-the-Wind was hungry enough to think that the simple stew that Lily prepared tasted almost as good as the shark and seafood celebration they shared on the beach.

She watched as Taelo, and Golden Hawk tied a series of poles to form a reinforcing zig-zag pattern on the perimeter poles.

This raised her concern. It seemed that Taelo was expecting a major challenge.

Then she saw Marigold riding hard toward the compound and yelled for the gate to be opened.

Not seeing Saber Scar, worried Feather-in-the-Wind. She shouted to keep the gate open for Saber Scar and ran to help Marigold.

She went back to the gate while the rest of the team unloaded and strategically placed the wood.

As she stood next to Marigold waiting for Saber Scar a steady solid rain began to fall. Then Golden Hawk pointed out Saber Scar being pursued by a very large number of huge wolves.

She stood aside as Taelo, and the stronger members of the team rushed forward to put up and secure the gate as Saber Scar rode into the compound.

She joined Quiet Rabbit, Busy Bee, and Lily as they let stones fly from their slings at the oncoming wolf pack.

The barrage of stones stopped the wolf pack for a short period.

Then the pack ran toward them and seemed to ignore the barrier. The front line hit the barrier, and some came almost halfway through and were snarling and snapping as they tried to push the rest of the way in.

She and the rest of the team smashed the skulls of any wolf that had its head through the wall. She was amazed that, though dead wolves formed a continuous ring around the perimeter, the other wolves kept attacking.

She agreed with Taelo when he pointed out that the wolves must never have met an adversary they did not defeat with their combined attack.

She watched as Saber Scar helped Golden Hawk pulled down the perimeter wall that had been pulled free from an anchor boulder by three wolves simultaneously hitting the barrier.

This demonstrated to her the power of the wolves and reinforced her trust of Taelo's preparation.

One wolf made it through, and it was attacked by Lasher, Walker and Arrow. The attacking wolf was bigger than all three combined.

Running Stag ran over to them and told Lasher and the rest to let the wolf go. Then, as the wolf ran at him, he took a swift step to the side and smashed the wolf's skull with his war hammer. She was surprised at the loud crack as she watched the wolf fall dead.

Taelo complemented Running Stag on his bravery.

She gave a small laugh when Taelo followed up with, "and don't do it again. As he gave Running Stag a hug".

An eerie atmosphere enveloped the compound as the wolf pack backed away, daylight faded, and the rain continued to make them all wet and miserable.

She took in the large number of dead wolves and noticed that the pack had positioned itself on the far side of the river.

Taelo commented that they were lucky to have the perimeter wall up when they were attacked.

She agreed with Golden Hawk's comment that luck had little to do with it and said that "It was all due to Taelo, the slave driver".

She was exhausted. And she was ravenous.

Lily offered everyone a piece of dried salted shark meat

Taelo decided that they should skin the wolves and throw the carcasses across the river at the wolves that seemed to have decided to spend the night there.

She was amazed as she watched Saber Scar swing a wolf's body and throw it across the river. No one else on the team had that strength.

She watched as Running Stag shot an arrow at any wolf that showed itself. He shot at least a dozen arrows.

She knew he had killed one because it was visible on the far bank. The wolf skinning went on for most of the night.

The central fire was burning, and the good smell of some food cooking attracted her. She ate some of the stew Lily had prepared and then after taking off her wet garments she crawled into her sleeping hide.

Always an early riser, Feather-in-the-Wind awoke before the rest of the team. The steady rain was still falling, and the heavy grey sky made it look like evening. She could not tell what time in the morning it might be.

She relieved a very tired Lily that had prepared enough fish stew to feed the entire team.

After getting up and feeding their mounts, Taelo and Running Stag went out across the river to see where the wolves were.

Later after their return she listened as Taelo praised Running Stag with having killed fourteen wolves and having retrieved all his shark toothed arrows.

This by Taelo's account made Running Stag the top wolf killer.

The rain stopped and the sky cleared.

The team had killed seventy wolves at the perimeter wall. Running Stag had killed fifteen with arrows and the sixteenth inside the compound with his war hammer.

Saber Scar and Running Stag took their mounts to drag the wolf carcasses farther way. She and the rest of the team hung the wolf hides on the compound's perimeter and scrapped them.

For the next twelve sun cycles, Feather-in-the-Wind took every opportunity to escape the scrapping, rubbing and drying work of the wolf hides. These wolves were at least twice as big as the dire wolves they knew. Processing their hides represented a great deal of work.

The team was ready to move on. The travois being pulled by the pack mounts were fully loaded.

Feather-in-the-Wind commented that the hide of the next rabbit she killed might require that another travois be used.

Chapter 7:

Feather-in-the-Wind enjoyed the morning sun and knew that by late afternoon a rain would follow. Then a cool clear evening would follow. This had been happening for the last few sun cycles.

She also registered the mountains receding toward the west and diminishing in size. The forest had thinned, and the underbrush punctuated by a new tall limbless tree with a burst of long leaves at the top became the cover of a flat plain. Closer examination also revealed a fruit that grew in clusters hanging down from between the leaves of the limbless tree.

Feather-in-the-Wind climbed one of these trees and cut the entire stem of hanging fruits down. The large green fruit proved to have a thick husk that once removed, exposed a hard nut. Three dark spots on one end were easily penetrated and a delicate and refreshing liquid was enjoyed by the entire team.

The sea birds once again greeted the team and the air spoke of the odor of the sea. Not long after, Feather-in-the-Wind observed the waves and realized that the rhythm of the waves was similar to the waves they had experienced in the North. The team had traveled South for several moons but were still next to sea they had first encountered in the North

The land leading to the sea was very different from their experience to the North. There the coastline was rocky, with coves featuring small beaches. Here in the south, it seemed that the beach was endless in both the northward and southward directions.

Most of the ground water the team experienced was brackish. They decided to make camp by a spring that had cold sweet water bubbling up from below. The spring formed a small stream that flowed into a large brackish swamp area.

Feather-in-the-Wind jumped in and slowly let herself float along the stream. The cold water made her gasp and she let out a yell. Once she reached the edge of the swamp she got back on the land and ran back to the spring. She soon had most of the team copying her antics. It was a warm day punctuated by riding the cool clear water of the stream several spear throws and then warming up on the walk back upstream.

Taelo declared that they had found their camp for their stay in this area. The sea was a short ride away, their spring water was fresh and cool, and the air warm and enjoyable.

Feather-in-the-Wind came back to set up her sleeping area and then joined in the preparation of a late meal. She contributed six rabbits that she had killed with her sling.

This was added to the rabbits that Quiet Rabbit, Busy Bee and Lily had bagged. Each member of the team was able to enjoy a salt and honey roasted rabbit.

As was usually the case Saber Scar and Marigold each had two. They were the most powerful two people on the team, and they required more food than the rest of the team. Both of them knew this and made a special effort to contribute as much to the food supply as possible.

Feather-in-the-Wind retired to her sleeping hide and stared up into the black night sky that was filled with countless points of light. Some were bright and some were dim and seemed distant.

She had listened to Saber Scar and Marigold describe their clan's interpretation of the lights. They admitted that they did not know what the lights were.

They asked a simple question, "We here on the land are so few and the lights in the sky are so many.

How could that be?"

"It does not matter how we think about the many points of light. The beauty and wonder awes us and the questions they raise cause us to think and improve ourselves," Quiet Rabbit commented.

Early the next morning, Feather-in-the-Wind opened her eyes as she heard Lily blowing on the coal to light the fire. She could hear the mounts, staked out at the edge of the camp, cutting, and munching on the grass. She looked up into the early morning sky and saw the eagle.

She watched the eagle circle the camp and fly to the West. Even before Taelo said a word, she knew that he would be telling the team that it was time to continue their journey.

That sun cycle, the team loaded the travois and continued their journey.

Feather-in-the-Wind continued to assault the rabbit population. She was constantly challenging one of the team to a contest of who could bag the most game. She seldom lost the contest and Lily always had an ample supply of ground hog, rabbit, squirrel and periodically some pigeon to use in preparing the one fresh meal the team always enjoyed when they made their camp at sundown.

The digging sticks Taelo and Golden Hawk had given everyone were constantly in use and Lily also had tubers, onions, and garlic to season the meat or to roast as separate treats.

Feather-in-the-Wind did less digging because she was always on the alert for small game when one of the other team members dismounted to dig for a plant.

She was pleased when sea birds once again greeted the team.

The birds led them to where calm water separated them from the land beyond. Golden Hawk verified that the water was salty. She volunteered to cross to the other side.

Taelo accepted but asked Running Stag to be her partner in the crossing.

She was pleased to have company for the crossing. Her mount proceeded out and soon it was swimming slowly toward the other side. It found footing and she and Running Stag rode out to the top of the grass covered sand dune. They called back that it was a sea, but it was different than the one they had just left.

Feather-in-the-Wind and Running Stag returned to the inner side. Taelo called out for them to stay on that side. He asked them to find a good place for the team to set up camp.

She and Running Stag rode their mount along the northside of the land. They came to a point where a large inner cove was formed. They crossed a dip in the land as they rode to the sea. The wind died down and it was calm. It was a good location that was shielded from the wind blowing in from the sea by a high sand dune and shielded from the north by a similar rise.

Feather-in-the-Wind rode back to the cove on the northside and walked out into the hip deep water. She then road back to the sea. She marveled at the bright white sand that made her squint. It reminded her of the winter snow when she had to wear eye coverings with thin slits in them to keep from being blinded.

She then went back to the crossing and met Quiet Rabbit and Lily as they crossed. She listened as Quiet Rabbit described a huge fish with a hammer head she had just seen.

Taelo spotted the huge fish and it turned out to be a shark almost as large as the one that he and Golden Hawk had killed in the Cove up north.

She and Running Stag led the team back to the site she and Running Stag had selected.

Taelo voiced his appreciation for a job well done. He then asked who wanted to go fishing in the shallow cove. Half of the team took him up on going fishing.

He asked Saber Scar to sit at the top of the hill that looked down at the small cove. He was to look out for the hammer head sharks.

Feather-in-the-Winds chuckled when Saber Scar said he liked his role looking for versus being in the water with the monsters.

Taelo put each person in position along a line that was to walk across the small bay at an angle that would drive the fish inward toward shore.

She was please that she had the position closest to the shore.

Quiet Rabbit stepped on an oyster and let everyone know what she had found.

Soon, Feather-in-the-Wind's bag was full of oysters.

Taelo lifted a spear and displayed a flat fish. He described what it looked like when it was on the bottom. It had one eye that seemed to look and the second eye on the bottom side seemed to look somewhat forward.

Knowing what to look for, Feather-in-the-Wind soon speared one of her own. She noted that all the team members in the water were bending down to pick up clams and spearing fish. She knew that Marigold and Lily would have plenty of food to cook.

Feather-in-the-Wind's foot came down on an object that struggled to get away. Even as she let out a scream, her spear plunged into the water. She was half crying and half laughing as she lifted her spear.

She lifted a still wiggling, three-foot long, hammer head shark. She declared she was done fishing since she did not want to meet its mother. She kept looking over her shoulder as she walked towards the shore.

Taelo agreed with her and told everyone to turn and walk slowly toward the shore.

She listened to Taelo as he joked about Saber Scar not telling her about the shark as a way, to test of her courage.

Saber Scar replied that it might be big enough to have eaten her but then the rest of the team would have been safe.

She enjoyed the teasing. She also knew that she did not want to meet such a beast when it was the size of the shark that had attacked Golden Hawk.

Golden Hawk volunteered to carry the small shark. He said he was interested in the placement of the eyes out at the end of the parts that made the "hammer".

That evening after the sumptuous feast, he brought up the shark. He commented about all the different forms animals seemed to take.

Busy Bee commented that the hammer head scared her but the monster that she had seen when she and Golden Hawk gathered the poles to make the raft horrified her. It was worse than all the tigers, lions, wolves, bears, and sharks rolled into one.

Feather-in-the-Wind replied that her experience stepping on the shark was all she could handle for the day.

For the next six sun cycles the team moved west along the beach. She, like all the team members took turns leading the four mounts pulling the travois. Marigold had pointed out that the sand at the edge of the sea provided the best footing for the mounts.

She and the rest of the team alternated riding their mounts along the shoreline or on top of the sand dune where the breeze seemed to reach its full strength.

The team reached the end of the beach. She watched as Taelo was the first to cross back to the north side. She was looking for the hammerheads, but she did not see any.

This time she and Running Stag were the last to go across.

Chapter 8:

Feather-in-the-Wind stood on the back her mount. She looked back to the glaring white of the beach sand, at the waves rolling energetically into shore. She admired the graceful flight of the sea birds as they rode the air and searched the beach and shallow water for their morning meals. She and Running Stag were the last to leave the beach area.

She had decided to stand up on her mount so that she could look down into the clear blue water between the island and the mainland shore. Her experience of stepping on and then spearing a small hammer head shark made her wary of this crossing. She and Running Stag had been the first to see the hammerheads when at the far end they had crossed over to the beach area.

At that time, they did not know of the existence of such a beast.

Now, she and Running Stag were last to cross because she wanted to keep a close watch as the rest of the team led the mounts and floated the team's belonging across.

She would sound the alarm and she knew she would ride in and attack any on coming hammerhead.

"I'm crazy," she thought.

Taelo and Golden Hawk had gone first and had taken most of the mounts across. Lily, Quiet Rabbit and Busy Bee had been the second group to cross.

These crossing were uneventful.

Burley Bear and Marigold each took one of the rafts loaded with the team's possessions. Feather-in-the-Wind was impressed with the strength they displayed. She watched both Marigold's and Saber Scar's arm muscles bulge as each pulled on a rope tied by Quiet Rabbit to a tree on the far side. Neither seemed to be strained by a load that she knew she would not be able to budge.

Their crossing was also uneventful.

Still standing on the back of her mount she nudged her into the water. She was surprised that her standing position was so stable. She urged Running Stag to get across first. As her mount cleared the water she sat down.

No hammerhead!

She rode over and dismounted as the team worked together to assemble and load the four travois.

She liked riding point. It allowed her to use her sling to down an occasional pigeon and bag a much greater number of rabbits and groundhogs.

One at a time various members of the team would join her. They almost always joked with her about her reacting just a bit slower so they could have a chance to use their sling.

She enjoyed the company of both Quiet Rabbit and Busy Bee the most. They would often come up to ride point together. When they did, Feather-in-the-Wind would ride in the middle and watch. She considered both to be true masters at the sling. Their smooth relaxed use of the sling from either side of their bodies let her know that she still had much to learn and to perfect.

The day had grown warm and the air rich in moisture. They all missed the fresh breeze cooling them on their beach ride. The team came to a swampy area that was bordered by a small river. The sun was close to the far horizon. There would be ample time to set up camp and then to prepare a good meal.

Golden Hawk wondered how close the team was to the mighty river.

Feather-in-the-Wind felt excitement as Quiet Rabbit and Busy Bee opened the hide where they kept the teams travel record. It was the first time they had willingly displayed it to the team. Feather-in-the-Wind always peeked over their shoulders when they worked on the travel record.

Now, she listened as Busy Bee clarified what she was showing. She credited Talking Wren with suggesting such a record. She, Quiet Rabbit and Talking Wren had drawn a faint series of circles. The center of the hide was the center of all the circles.

The journey started at the top left edge of the outer most circle. Then a line came down at an angle about a third of the way down and close to the middle where a dark thick line represented the mighty river. A second not quite as heavy line slanted from a point just below the first downward angled line and then angled back upward to the East. Then it met the eastern mountains. It followed a small stream through the mountains and then on the top edge of the hide stopped at the ocean.

Feather-in-the-Wind then followed the line down along the side of the markings that indicated the mountains and finally once again out to the ocean. A dark wiggly line indicated the coastline, but it lacked detail.

The cross over to the white sand beaches and the long thin piece of land with water on both sides was easy to understand.

The map stopped at the small river where they were camped.

She marveled at the small figures that illustrated key events experienced at each location. At the beginning point was the white of the mountain snows. This was followed by the buffalo hunt they had done before arriving at the Grazing Elk Clan. At the Grazing Elk Clan was a pack of wolves that they had left behind.

Then she felt a pang as she took in the figures, clearly it was she and Running Stag when they discovered Paradise Falls. Quit rabbit had even put in the mist generated by the falls. This she knew was the place that he had captured her heart and where she had given her heart. The valley filled with mounts captivated her as well.

She felt her guilt rise up as she took in the giant bear hugging the figure, that she knew to be Taelo. A small figure was depicted looking down from the top of a large pine. She smiled they had captured the mood of the moment exactly as she felt it.

Next was the giant clawed beasts being watched by the team and the team being watched by lions.

Then she was again shown as a small figure pointing to the gap in the mountains. She was standing next to a person she knew to be Quiet Rabbit.

The top view of a gigantic shark attacking Golden Hawk with a figure holding a spear diving down from the cliff was magnificent.

She was again featured as she danced on the singing sand beach. Running Stag was featured in a stance with his arrow pulled back as he shot at the giant wolves.

Where they had stopped in their southernmost point, she was shown floating away from the spring and floating down the stream.

Next came the hammer head shark. There was the image of the hammer head and another of a figure holding up a spear with a hammer head.

The long white beach, with waves and birds brought her to the end.

To say she was impressed would not do justice to the work before her. The skill, the ability to capture the essence and the mood, the subtle application of color was beyond what Feather-in-the-Wind could imagine. She let out a whoosh of air and gave Quiet Rabbit and Busy Bee a hug and whispered a thank you.

Feather-in-the-Wind stepped back and complemented them and let them know how impressed she was.

Then she repeated Golden Hawk's question, "How far are we from the mighty river"?

Busy Bee replied that she was not totally sure but most likely they were one or two sun cycles to the east.

She looked at the rest of the team and asked if anyone wanted to make a bet on how many sun cycles would pass before they reached the mighty river.

Lily had been tracing the team's route on the hide with her finger. When she arrived at their current location, she replied that she estimated three sun cycles to the river.

Running Stag pointed to one small black figure with large bright yellow eyes at the other end of the white sand beach and asked about it.

Busy Bee commented that it was the monster she had seen when she and Golden Hawk had been gathering logs for the raft.

Running Stag voiced his hope that they would not meet that beast.

They had traveled northward along the river and their current camp was at a point where the river was the narrowest.

Taelo asked Running Stag to ride across and check on the river's depth. Feather-in-the-Wind noted that the water was just up to the mount's belly. She figured that the water was not very deep.

She went hunting with her sling but came back with only a couple of rabbits.

She was very happy with the sack full of frogs that Saber Scar and Golden Hawk had bagged during their search for some river rapids that would make the crossing easier. They had found no rapids but a great number of large, sleepy frogs.

Taelo had set up a fish trap that had yielded a handful of large fish.

"I really enjoy preparing food for this team. We always seem to eat well, and we always have something new and unique," Lily said as she turned the spits holding the frog legs and the fish.

The rabbit meat went to Lasher, Arrow and Bold Walker.

The one ground hog Feather-in-the-Wind had bagged was coated with salt and honey and roasted on its own spit.

As predicted by Lily their meal was delicious.

Early on the next sun cycle the team crossed the muddy river and proceeded on their way through a wet marshy land. They came to a second small river when suddenly Golden Hawk and his mount stopped and backed away. Busy Bee's monster was laying asleep on the bank of the river. Its body was as long as two mounts and almost as wide as she was tall.

Feather-in-the-Wind asked if she should use her sling to wake it.

"Let sleeping monsters sleep," Taelo commented.

Marigold went on to point out two more of the monsters on the far side of the river.

As the team began to cross, Feather-in-the-Wind watched as the two monsters downstream of the team entered the water. Quiet Rabbit pointed out several more upstream. Lily the last of the team to cross was leading the four pack mounts pulling the travois.

Feather-in-the-Wind observed the giant monster sleeping on the shore come awake as Lilly went by.

The monster came out of the water in fast pursuit of Lily then turned and pursued her and the mounts as she urged her mount to move faster.

The stones from Feather-in-the-Wind's sling had no effect on the beast. Hitting it on the eyes seemed to have slowed it enough for Lily to reach the rest of the team but it came constantly forward toward the team.

She watched as the beast focused its attack on Golden Hawk. Saber Scar attacked from the side and drove his spear just behind the monster's head, down into the ground. The monster's tail hit him full force and threw him through the air into the brush as if he were weightless.

The force had launched Saber Scar a large heavy powerful person. A person Feather-in-the-Wind could not imagine being able to lift, was hurled six spear lengths through the air!

Taelo and Golden Hawk plunged their spears in from the side. The beast was still trying to attack. Busy Bee drove her spear in just behind the beast's left leg in an attempt to hit the heart.

Quiet Rabbit came behind Busy Bee and drove her spear into the same area and pushed both spears in farther.

Taelo leaped across and saved Quiet Rabbit from the tail.

The tail almost caught her.

Marigold came in with Saber Scar's war hammer, straddled the beast as if it was her mount and with all her strength repeatedly smashed the monster between the eyes. She relentlessly delivered powerful blow after powerful blow. The monster's head turned into a smashed bloody mess.

Except for a slight twitch the monster's tail stopped its movement.

She heard Taelo casually commenting that the team should never make Marigold mad.

She joined in as in unison the team quietly repeated, "don't make Marigold mad".

A dazed Saber Scar got up and wondered what had happened. Feather-in-the-Wind and the rest of the team were surprised he had no broken bones or seemingly any other injury.

He accepted Marigolds help in walking over to look at the dead monster.

Feather-in-the-Wind appreciated Taelo recognizing Saber Scar for his bravery and saving the team by pinning the monster to the ground. That single act had probably saved them all.

She later she watched as Busy Bee and Quiet Rabbit opened their travel hide and drew a larger, clearer picture of Busy Bee's monster.

After skinning the monster, quickly scrapping its hide, and salting and wrapping the tail flesh for a later meal, the team continued on.

Lily was correct on her estimate. Three sun cycles later they stopped on the banks of the mighty river.

She and the team agreed when Taelo suggested they make the crossing immediately. They assembled their rafts and floated across to the western side.

Quiet Rabbit announced that they were now only one section of her journey map away from completing their journey.

A few sun cycles later, Feather-in-the-Wind was in the lead when Golden Hawk returned from scouting ahead. He announced that a very stranger creature that seemed to have an armor for its skin was just ahead.

She followed Taelo and the team and watched as Lasher, Bold Walker and Arrow all circled the giant, armor plate scaled animal. It came to a halt and seemed to take no action. It was as tall as the mount she was on and almost as long. The fact that it ignored the wolves and then slowly moved on reassured her that it was non-aggressive. She rode her mount next to the slowly moving animal to feel the texture of it covering. She was impressed by how thick it seemed when she poked it with the tip of her spear.

Since the huge but seemingly gentle beast was traveling in the direction the team was going. Taelo and the team followed.

It was not long until the giant approached an ant filled mound. It used a set of formidable claws to dig a hole into the mound and then a long snake like tongue went into the hole and was pulled back with ants sticking on it.

After a few moments of watching, Feather-in-the-Wind suggested they move on.

The team traveled northward until Marigold declared that the river ahead of them was the one the team had earlier followed east to the Mighty River.

Feather-in-the-Wind had ridden ahead with Running Stag and located a good campsite. She was eager to return to the place they called Paradise.

Feather-in-the-Wind: The Eastern Elk Clan

Chapter 9:

The team followed the river westward. The tall green grasses mixed with a variety of wildflowers slowly gave way to one of pines, oak and maple trees seemingly harboring the still prevalent grasses.

Feather-in-the-Wind took advantage of the increased rabbit and small game population. It was clear to the rest of the team that they would eat well on her success with the sling.

Finally, they arrived at a familiar point where a smaller stream flowing from the north entered the larger river. Lasher was as eager to cross over as she was.

Taelo smiled and said that she could accompany Lasher.

She, Running Stag and Lasher, Arrow and Bold Walker all entered the river at the same time.

Lasher and the other two wolves ran ahead but Feather-in-the-Wind kept her mount at a slow walk.

She reached over and took Running Stag's hand as she rode.

She closed her eyes and listened as the breeze rustled the leaves of the willows along the stream's banks. She looked down into the stream at the fish slowly undulating as they stayed in position and even spotted a large crayfish sitting on a flat stone beneath the water basking in the sunlight. She let the forest speak to her and the dry grasses caressed her mounts legs. This was a place that would always be in her memory. This she thought was a perfect ending to a perfect trip.

Then she looked to the northwest. The setting sun burnt a red edge on the lower front edge of the dark black approaching clouds. This fiery edge evoked the image of a hot blade ready to cut the flesh. Its fast movement threatened the team who rode their mounts in with urgency.

The mood changed from pleasure at having returned to one of rushed work to fend off disaster.

Feather-in-the-Wind took control of all the mounts as she and Lily staked them out along the stream where they could feed.

She then joined the rest of the team in gathering the materials to make a lodge. She led the team to a bank along the stream that had some flat stone that would serve as digging stones.

She stopped and pointed to the base of the water fall and the rainbow mix of colors created by the setting sun. The dark almost black approaching clouds and the gorgeous display colors at the falls seemed to be a contrast between good and evil.

All of the next sun cycle she and Running Stag and several of the team gathered stones to make the primary wall for the exposed part of the lodge the team was building. They positioned the stones and closed the gaps with a mixture of wet dirt and grass.

Feather-in-the-Wind and Running Stag collected wood from the surrounding area. They put the pile to the side of the lodge so it would be easily accessible for both the internal warming fire and the external cooking fire.

She was amazed at how quickly the team, working together, was able to build the lodge. The finishing touches were being put on when the dark clouds that had threatened them throughout the day delivered huge snowflakes that fell on them like a hide being dropped across an open entryway. The snow came down in fist sized chunks. It was dangerous to stand outside the lodge.

She and several of the team ran out with hides to put over the mounts.

She knew that they had completed their effort just in time. She helped Lily make a small fire at the entrance to the lodge. And appreciated the grilled piece of salted dear meat and a leg of rabbit.

She agreed with Busy Bee when she expressed her exhaustion. Feather-in-the-Wind went to her sleeping hide and crawled in.

The snow continued for most of the next sun cycle. She went out to tend to the mounts and was surprised at how well they had tamped down the snow. She watched as Taelo, Golden Hawk and Running Stag rode across the river.

After making sure all the mounts were fed, she returned to the lodge to pack her belongings. She planned to be ready when Taelo returned. She was eager to capture more mounts.

"The excellent work done by Feather-in-the-Wind and Running Stag last season to mark the trail to the valley of the mounts is now going to save us much time. Their black feathered flags on top of their marker poles go out as far as the eye can see," Taelo commented on his return.

Both Feather-in-the-Wind and Running Stag beamed at the praise. They had wanted to make trail markers that would be there for a longtime and now their work was going to help the team get out of a tough situation.

The sky was clear, but the weather was a piercing cold that crept in through their thick coats as they rode through the deep snow toward the west.

"I think I could use two more bearskin coats," Feather-in-the-Wind commented. She had on all the warm clothing she could possibly put on and she was still cold.

They followed the poles marking the way to the valley of the mounts. The snow had almost filled the valley, but Taelo and Golden Hawk found the herd of horses trapped and surrounded by snow about three spears deep.

"Our flat shark toothed weapons make good shovels," Feather-in-the-Wind commented when they talked about digging through the snow.

"Yes, and I brought several of the flat digging stones along to use when cooking," Lily volunteered.

Feather-in-the-Wind was assigned to be on one of the three digging teams. The removed snow was transported on a large hide to an area away from the digging site. She and her mount pulled the hide loaded with snow and deposited it on an ever-growing mountain.

When Saber Scar excitedly cried out that he had broken through to the mounts, Feather-in-the-Wind let out a shout of relief from the top of the snow pile that looked like a small mountain.

There were more than forty mounts to choose from. Sixteen were selected and culled out. The rest were left behind and would be able to leave as they desired.

The selected mounts seemed to accept the situation more quickly than the original first group. Perhaps it was that they were in a worn-out condition, or the tamed mounts provided a calming effect.

Taelo called for the team to move on immediately. He emphasized that everyone should bundle up and stay warm and that the temperature was the coldest he had ever experienced.

"I can't hear you," Feather-in-the-Wind called out. She was on her mount and had pulled an additional hide around and over her heavy winter parka.

"And we can't see you," Quiet Rabbit replied jokingly.

Some bison were spotted, and the team decided to send out three teams to down three buffalo.

Feather-in-the-Wind watched as Taelo, and Golden Hawk downed the ones they had selected. She then reacted with concern as she watched as Saber Scar was thrown off his mount and hit the side of the buffalo he was pursuing. She gave a sigh of relief when Saber Scar dusted off the snow and checked out his mount.

Taelo came back and joked that Saber Scar was supposed to throw his spear at the buffalo and not try to be a Feather-in-the-Wind.

Marigold commented that she heard the buffalo laughing as it got up and trotted away.

Feather-in-the-Wind gave Saber Scar a hug and told him not to listen to anyone but her. She thought he had great form in how he hit the buffalo and that he had succeeded in knocking it down! She commented that he would have been successful if Marigold would have been quicker with her war hammer.

The team enjoyed a good laugh at the banter and then all joined in to skin the two buffalo and later enjoy the grilled meat prepared by Lily.

Four sun cycles later they arrived at the Eastern Elk Clan village. No sooner had they settled in when they were asked for assistance in locating the missing group of hunters. The main hunters for the Eastern Elk Clan had not returned when expected.

She and Running Stag went along on the rescue mission. They remained out in the valley that had been trampled and cleared by a passing buffalo herd. They were to hold all the mounts but were to ride away if attacked by the dire wolves that the team had encountered.

Running Stag and Feather-in-the-Wind moved the mounts out toward the center of the bison pathway. A short time later Feather-in-the-Wind pointed to two very large animals coming toward them.

"I think the wolves have found us," Feather-in-the-Wind said as she pointed to the oncoming wolves.

"Let's get ready to ride. I want to get a couple of arrows into them before we turn and run," Running Stag said as he dismounted and got his bow ready.

His first arrow found its mark and went at least halfway in. The second also found its mark on the second oncoming wolf. Two more shots put two more arrows into the oncoming wolves.

"Well so much for following instructions and riding away," Feather-in-the-Wind said in a relieved voice.

"Keep an eye out for more of them," Running Stag said as he pulled out his arrows and cleaned them.

He then took out his knife and proceeded to skin the two wolves.

Running Stag had just finished skinning the two dire wolves when high in the sky an eagle let out a long cry.

"I am not sure what the eagle cry is for but let's be ready to ride or to give help," Feather-in-the-Wind said as she looked up into the sky.

"Let's drag these two to the edge of the trail. Perhaps it will give the other wolves a second thought," Running Stag said as he tied the rope to the back legs of the skinned wolves.

The two had just finished when Taelo and Golden Hawk came charging out of the forest with a pack of dire wolves on their heels.

The two flew out onto the bison trail and ran toward Running Stag standing with his bow ready. Feather-in-the-Wind had the mounts ready to ride and two spears to hand out.

Running Stag stood and rapidly shot his arrows at the oncoming wolves. This time he shot for the wolves' mouths. The arrows hit their mark and the arrows went through and cut the spine. One after another the wolves dropped in their tracks.

Running Stag had six kills before Taelo, and Golden Hawk turned with spears in hand.

Suddenly with a loud cry, she rode in from the side and bashed two of the wolves in the head with her war hammer. She had removed her coat and was riding with no hands on her mount.

The battle continued for only a short period. Taelo and Golden Hawk used their spears and war hammers to kill several of the wolves, but she and Running Stag and that made the difference. They each had a half dozen kills.

"You two make a deadly pair," Taelo said as he helped Running Stag retrieve his arrows.

The rescue of the hunters was a blur of action. She and Running Stag led the mounts back into the rescue area and then led the way out.

Over her shoulders she could see Running Stag, Taelo and Golden Hawk dropping pieces of meat to the pursuing dire wolves.

She remembered Taelo's words of thanks for not having followed his instructions but instead using their judgement of what to do when they were first attacked.

She truthfully admitted that it had been Running Stag that had decided that the wolves were probably faster than their mounts. He thought it best to stand and fight.

This incident was the final connection between her and Running Stag. He was brave and willing to face the situation. He consistently demonstrated his fighting skill and always out fought his opponent. He was humble and never boasted.

On that sun cycle she decided that he was a treasure to be cherished.

Chapter 10

Their return to the Grazing Elk Clan village with all the hunters was highly celebrated. Many had feared the worst and were overwhelmed in their relief. An impromptu celebration in honor of Taelo and his team occurred.

"I can tell you that the stories of the hunter's trials, their belief that they were doomed, and your team's incredibly brave rescue will be told to all this coming clan gathering," Lily commented the day after the celebration.

"Our success was due to our ability to work together and to each act individually when it was needed.

Running Stag's decision to kill the two dire wolves instead of running meant he and Feather-in-the-Wind were there to help when Golden Hawk and I ran out ahead of the pack chasing us.

Feather-in-the-Wind's unbelievable riding skills and courage was another key action that ended the pursuit.

Running Stag's accuracy with his bow saved the day.

The rest of the team got the wounded hunters ready to ride.

The strength of Saber Scar made it possible for the wounded hunters to be put on the mounts.

Each hunter had to be held as we escaped the chase of the remaining dire wolves.

After our return Marigold, Quiet Rabbit and Busy Bee tended to the wounded hunters.

Let the rescued hunters tell the story of their recovery.

Make sure the team gets credit in the stories that will be told," Taelo extemporized so all could hear.

Feather-in-the-Wind went out on several buffalo hunts as the team provided the Grazing Elk Clan enough meat to last until spring and until their hunters had recovered and could once again hunt.

The thrill of running past the buffalo to set the spear for them to impale themselves on never ceased to thrill her. This way of hunting meant that her speed not her size determined her success.

Taelo brought up continuing their journey. He suggested going first to the Elk Clan in the Valley of Plenty. Then they would proceed to the cave of the Clan of Others and finally they would complete their journey by traveling to the valley where the Northern Elk Clan was located.

Feather-in-the-Wind had trained many the Grazing Elk Clan in the use of the sling. She trained others on how to tame the mount. She had enjoyed her stay but was eager to complete the journey.

A moon cycle later the team arrived to the Valley of Plenty and the Elk Clan.

Taelo asked her to ride in standing on her mount.

Golden Hawk and Busy Bee rode in on their mounts leading one mount for each of their parents.

To Feather-in-the-Wind's surprise Running Stag brought his mount next to hers and stood up and rode into the valley standing beside her. She looked over at him and saw that he wore a beaming smiling. He had not told her that he had learned to stand on his mount.

The story telling went on almost all night. Giving rides on the mounts went from sunrise to sunset. Then it was time to go north to the home of the Clan of Others.

The hot water pool with the rain maker was all that Feather-in-the-Wind could think about. Such a luxury was something most clans could only imagine and dream of.

Broken Spear, the seer of the Clan had predicted the team's arrival.

Once again, Feather-in-the-Wind and Running Stag rode toward the gathering of the clan members standing on their mounts. She did a flip and glanced over at Running Stag to see if he would do one. He laughed and shook his head.

The hot tub was just as delicious to her bones as she had imagined. She sat under the warm water rain and closed her eyes.

Much too soon she was urged to come out because the main evening celebration was about to start.

She along with everyone else enjoyed the stories told by Taelo, Golden Hawk, Saber Scar and Marigold.

The story about Marigold getting revenge on the long-tailed monster made the phrase, "Don't make Marigold mad," a chant taken up by all the Clan of Others. They repeated it multiple times throughout the story telling.

Too Soon it was time to travel on.

Two sun cycles of travel brough the sight of the twin snow-covered mountains in to view. Only the team's previous experience let them rediscover the small frozen lake now totally covered by a thick layer of snow.

Always a favorite place, it once again served as the point to stop and prepare for the next short leg of the trip up the river to the branch leading back to the valley and the lodge of the Northern Elk Clan.

The team was now down to two pack mounts and six gift mounts.

Floating Cloud, who had decided to accompany her granddaughter, Quiet Rabbit, insisted she take care of the pack mounts.

Lily had stayed in the Valley of Plenty where she had been approached by a suitor. She knew that this was most likely her last change at have a lifelong mate.

"It will be good to return to the Northern Elk Clan," Quiet Rabbit said.

She realized she thought of it as her home.

"Yes, I want to ride the valley and experience it in a new way," Feather-in-the-Wind added.

Quiet Rabbit and Feather-in-the-Wind tended to the mounts. Afterwards the two took their slings and hunted for rabbit. They were surprised by the number of rabbits and were able to bag two rabbits for each person and for Lasher, Arrow and Bold Walker.

"Does this team eat so well each time it stops," Floating Cloud asked as she tended to the roasting rabbits with the rest of the team.

"Only when Feather-in-the-Wind and Quiet Rabbit hunt together," Running Stag replied with a smile.

"Yes, in this whole journey, I do not recall a time when the team did not have a good to great dinner," Taelo replied.

"Oh, what about the times you cooked," Quiet Rabbit teased.

"Yes, I suppose you could blame me for some of the poorer dinners. Luckily, we had Lily there to save the day," Taelo replied with a coy smile.

The way the team always ate his meals gave him confidence in his cooking ability. He could take the joking.

The next sun cycle after cleaning up the camp and leaving it ready for the next visit, the team took up the last part of their journey.

From high in the sky came an eagle cry. It flew out ahead of them and later gave the same cry over the valley of the Northern Elk Clan.

"We have brought special gifts.

From the Elk Clan and the Valley of Plenty and Red Oak and Quiet Pheasant, we bring four mounts loaded with meat.

For White Swan and Gray Fox Running we have a mount each," Taelo said as he stepped back from hugs of both his parents, White Swan and Gray Fox Running.

Quiet Rabbit handed the ropes of each mount to White Swan and Gray Fox Running.

She had worked hard at taming each mount.

"And for my favorite parents, I bring you each a, mount," Running Stag said as he handed over the ropes to the two mounts he had been leading.

"And for all the rest of you to learn to ride, I bring two more mounts," Feather-in-the-Wind said from where she was standing on her mount.

The thought had just magically appeared.

She had been struggling as to whom she would give her mounts.

A cheer went up from the entire Northern Elk Clan.

"Well, I see our Feather-in-the-Wind has gained another new skill," White Swan commented as she watched the young woman ride standing on her mount around the edge of the ring formed by the clan members.

"I will give short rides to any person wanting to try," Feather-in-the-Wind volunteered as Taelo helped White Swan get on her mounted.

The rest of the sun cycle was spent giving rides to the eager clan members.

The warm memories of the Journey of Discovery played out as Feather-in-the-Wind sat waiting outside of the Leadership council meeting.

Running Stag sat down beside her and gave her a hug.

She looked at him and smiled. They had now been mates for more than twelve moon cycles.

Their bond grew stronger with each passing day.

The sun was setting as her mind wandered and recalled the team's journey North to the land of his origin.

Feather-in-the-Wind put her head on his shoulder, whispered his name and closed her eyes.

Chapter 11:

Feather-in-the-Wind let her mind free to remember this last trip the team had experienced. For this trip, the team ended up being much larger than previous journey teams. The true size only became known when meeting with the Clan of Others.

Lily and her newly acquired mate, Slow Runner had returned to join the team. She, Running Stag, Golden Hawk, Busy Bee, Quiet Rabbit, Floating Cloud, Quiet Rabbits grandmother and her friend Bashful Lark made up the team.

The mist generated by the water falling from the mighty height of the waterfall in the valley of the Northern Elk Clan came to her mind. The cold air froze the fine mist and turned it into fine delicate snowflakes that landed gently on the valley below. Each flake formed its unique, delicate, and beautiful pattern. It would drift down and land on top of the ever-growing mound below.

The water not turned into mist cascaded down from its height into the ice-covered pool, open where the water from above kept it from freezing. The water flowed, beneath an ice layer, into the small river that ran along the cliff's base past the clan's compound to join another stream and then flowed on toward the sea to the west.

This grand valley with its towering waterfall was the new home she had accepted. She had not forgotten the beauty of the mountains of her childhood in the land of the Condor, but she had accepted that she would never see that land again.

Her mind turned to the journey to the North.

Taelo had warned that the journey to the North would be the most challenging. She and the rest of the team were not dissuaded. It was clear that the team had high confidence in Taelo as their leader.

She listened as Lily shared how hard this journey would be for her. It would bring back the memories of her capture by the Cannibals and later having to watch as her mate was tortured and then devoured. It was a horror that would stay fresh to the end of her days. She was however going to support Taelo no matter her feelings.

"I know how she feels. Taelo has been my hero since the time he returned and freed my mother and father by killing the Cannibals holding them. I was very lucky. I know the pain and sorrow that Lily speaks of. It will be a tough trip for me as well but I have a Feather-in-the Wind to strengthen me," Running Stag said quietly.

"I am beginning to understand why Wise Owl created and gave the title of warriors at large to both Taelo and Golden Hawk. They have given each of us a second life.

I too understand the loss of family. Mine live on, but I can never return to the condor and the mountains to the South. But I have a new purpose and I will follow Taelo and Quiet Rabbit anywhere they wish to go," she replied to Running Stag.

Taelo's core team had continued their tradition of having a meal together once a week. They had found a comfortable location down by the river where they could sit and watch the sunset.

Once again it was Taelo's turn to cook. This time he was showboating. He had been out and was lucky enough to bag a young boar. He and Lasher had run it down and brought it back for this occasion.

He had sought out both Lily and Floating Cloud for cooking guidance and had carefully followed their advice.

"Well, both of you will know if I followed your detailed instructions well enough," he said as he turned away from the fire.

The coals had slowly cooked the honey basked young boar. The aroma was tantalizing. Everyone was eager to get a piece.

Feather-in-the-Wind looked around at Lily, Slow Runner, Floating Cloud, Bashful Lark, Quiet Rabbit, Golden Hawk, Busy Bee, and Running Stag. The rest of the team and members of the Others were yet to join. A feeling of joy welled up insider her.

Taelo shared his uneasy feeling about the trip. He planned to pay a visit to the Clan of Others and talk with Broken Spear. When he asked when the team should go there, she and the rest of the team all expressed the same sentiment, "As soon as possible."

She knew that all of them had the same vision of sitting in the hot spring pool located in the cave of the Others.

The trip south through the Twin Marker Mountains, down to the sea went smoothly. Lasher, Arrow and Bold Walker were the only wolves accompanying the team. Each walked beside their owner.

Lasher and Taelo were inseparable.

Arrow had a similar relationship with Running Stag and Bold Walker was devoted to her.

She was looking forward to reuniting with her friends.

They all walked to the edge of the sea and dipped their hands into the water.

"The water is still very, very cold, but even in the summer it remains cold," Busy Bee noted.

They walked on until the beach ended. Then the team went single file along the base of the cliff. This approach would bring them to the small stream that made its way to the sea from the cave of the Others.

"Look ahead and you will see our friend Burley Bear," Running Stag commented as he bolted ahead.

Feather-in-the-Wind saw both Burley Bear and Meadow Flower waiting and standing beside them were two other familiar friends, Saber Scar and Marigold.

She gave both Saber Scar and Marigold hugs and did the same with Burley Bear and Meadow Flower.

She felt a strong bond with all four. They had all played important roles in her rescue and later in her survival. There was a special relationship between her and these four of the Others.

She followed everyone back into the cave of the Others. She heard Taelo quietly commenting that some surprise was at hand. It was the first time that he and his team were so formally greeted.

After putting her things down in the area that they would sleep she went on to the meeting area. She always enjoyed the food served by the Others. Running Stag made a comment about how much she could eat and wondered where she put it.

Then the story telling was announced by Burley Bear. He announced that he would begin by telling the story of how he had met Taelo.

Feather-in-the-Wind was immediately interested. She knew the story and she knew that this was the first time Burley Bear would tell his version of the meeting of the two.

"I begin with the trickery the Elk Clan displayed the first time we encountered them. Our food shortage was severe. I was out hunting for deer or elk. Then I smelled the odor of smoking meat. I followed my nose to the edge of a cliff. Carefully I peered over the edge of the cliff at a hunting party of the new ones below.

They were drying strips of meat.

My mouth watered.

I am the largest among us, but you all know I am a ghost when I want to spy on someone. No one but Broken Spear has ever been able to see me coming.

Somehow the leader of the new ones sensed he was being watched. He sent out several scouts to determine if there was someone watching.

I quickly retreated back to our camp on the beach.

We all knew our camp was not in a good location, but Broken Spear had declared this was the location we would meet the person who would lead us on a new path.

We would meet the man of the Eagle.

On my return to camp, I organized a raiding party. I was determined we would get the meat this hunting party possessed.

Quiet Fox was not supportive of this venture, but he knew the clan was on the verge of starvation. He considered the alternatives and allowed me to take a team to see if we could steal the meat.

He gave strict orders not to kill anyone or even injure them.

This was a tough challenge for a raiding party.

We were brash and brave and knew we would come home with all the meat and be seen as heroes. We found a place down the beach and waited for the hunting party to appear.

"YES", we all whispered when the loaded travois being pulled by four warriors appeared. We waited until they had committed to their direction and then we came swooping out of the forest.

What a surprise. Even with the loaded travois the warriors were close to out running us. Slowly we gained on the travois they were pulling. When we were a spears throw away, the four dropped the travois and accelerated and disappeared into the woods.

We triumphantly turned the travois and hastily pulled them back to our beachside camp.

We were triumphant and were loud and brash in our boasting. We were thoroughly embarrassed when we took the cover off the load and realized the load was almost all wood with only a thin covering of meat.

Instead of being treated like heroes, we were greeted with laughter. The old warriors had their day pointing out to us the difference between a piece of wood and buffalo meat.

"Well, it seems you have met your match in trickery," Quiet Fox publicly praised me.

"Though I was angry, even I had a good laugh. Such trickery can only be admired.

I now know Red Oak the current leader of the Elk Clan was the person who planned the trick. The two of us have laughed together about that evening.

He has told me about how hard he found it to keep running while laughing to the point he had tears in his eyes. He and his men stopped at the edge of the woods and collapsed in laughter.

He told me that if we had been able to keep up with them, they would have surrendered in laughter.

The audience all let out a light whooping in appreciation of the story.

"So, you can understand how I felt later when two beautiful women and two scraggly boys trying to be warriors approached our camp. I looked up and down the beach and into the forest.

I knew this was another trick. I just could not figure out what kind of trick it might be.

Why would the new ones come to us with gifts?

Never before had any of the new ones even acknowledged our existence. The best treatment we ever received was to be left alone.

What could they possibly be up to?

I kept looking up the beach and into the forest. Something was up.

Immediately I knew these two were trying to find out what we were doing. They were spying.

I reached for the one that seemed to be in charge.

I was just going to get her attention.

Then…., Well then," Burley Bear stopped and looked slowly around, "…then the lights went out."

The whooping of the clan members was thunderous.

Burley Bear raised his hands into the air and slowly turned a circle.

"I woke up in my lodge. It took me a moment to recall where I was and who I was. I was furious. I came roaring out of my lodge to find the warrior that had blind-sided me.

As all of you know, no one in the clan has ever beaten me in combat.

What did I find?

There sitting next to Quiet Fox was a small, barely above my waist, boy.

Where was the warrior that had turned out the lights, I angrily shouted?

The boy stood up and put out his hand and said, "I am Taelo, claw of the eagle, the claw that strikes,"

Burley Bear clawed the air in an exaggerated motion and slowly turned with a grimace on his face.

The clan members were whooping as they watched Burley Bear.

"Then high in the sky, an eagle cried, and I realized that Broken Spear's prediction that the "Man of the Eagle" would come to guide the clan. His prediction had come true!"

I stopped in my tracks. At that moment I realized Taelo was to lead us to our new home.

You all know that Taelo made me see. He made me see new possibilities. He made me see new ways of doing things. He made me see a new future for our clan.

He found us our cave, he found us the whale and he has given us new purpose.

The audience was slapping the ground and whooping in appreciation of the story.

And now a story by Taelo, the claw that strikes," Burly Bear said as he sat down and urged Taelo to stand up.

Feather-in-the-Wind slapped the ground as hard as all the other listeners.

The story telling ended just before the sun came above the horizon.

Feather-in-the-Wind was slow to rise and went to the warm pool as soon as she arose. The yellow flowers growing from the roots of the large green leaves floating in the water at the lower end of the pool reminded her of the mountain lake to the South where they grew in abundance. Here they would only thrive in the warm water pool.

She watched as a mount with three riders was slowly making its way back to the cave. It was Broken Spear. He was sandwiched between his two attendants on what looked like a leather bundle that allowed him to see over the person in front of him.

"Good Morning. I see that you have been waiting for me in my morning meeting area," Broken Spear said in greeting as the three arrived.

Feather-in-the-Wind was about to respond when she realized that he was speaking to Taelo, who was also sitting in the warm water pool.

She overheard Broken Spear saying that Taelo would need a larger team on his journey North.

She then watched as Taelo, Broken Spear and Golden Hawk left the pool and walked over to where they would take their first meal. She watched as Burley Bear, Meadow Flower, Saber Scar and Marigold arrived. They introduced Sharp Blade and Single Leaf.

She almost slipped off her rock when Taelo signaled for her and
Running Stag to join the group. She and Running Stag looked at each
other and quietly found a place to sit.

She listened as Broken Spear began, "Yes, this is of my doing. I
wanted to talk to all of you at once. I have flown with the eagle and
have seen much of what is in your journey to the North.

On your *Journey of Discovery* to the East I spent many troubling
days with the ancients during the time Taelo was injured and visited
with them.

They know that on each of these journeys Taelo must deal with a
life and death situation. If he deals with it correctly, he lives. If he
deals with it poorly, he is likely to die," Broken Spear began.

"Our very first meal at this cave, with Taelo, was whale meat. I
saved some dried whale meat for these many seasons. We will have a
morning whale meat stew with seeds from Meadow Flower's yellow
flower and some milk from my own mount. The meal has been
seasoned and prepared by our best cooks," Broken Spear said as he
signaled his cooking team into action.

"I have not been able to see the most dangerous part of the journey
to the North. However, the situation was discussed among the ancients.
You must understand that though I was there in my mind, it was very
hard to directly converse with them.

Taelo was there as well and often spoke to them. Do you remember
your discussions with them," Broken Spear said as he looked toward
Taelo?

Feather-in-the-Wind was holding her breath as she waited for Taelo's response.

"This is something I have shared only with Quiet Rabbit," Taelo began as he looked around.

He absent-mindedly scratched Lasher behind his ears.

"Even then I have only shared a small portion of the discussions I had with the Ancients.

"I knew if I shared even a small part of my discussions with the Ancients, Golden Hawk would have had me bound to my mount for the remainder of the journey," Taelo said with a smile and a nod to his friend.

"Yes, I did discuss and argue the appropriate actions to take for many situations that they posed to me. It seemed to be a test of some sort. I was trying to make sense of it all when I awoke to Quiet Rabbit trying to feed me some of Lily's stew. I figured I had passed the test," Taelo continued

Feather-in-the-Wind had tended to Taelo a great deal of time during his recover. He had risked his life to save her from a giant bear. She felt his injuries were her fault. During this time, he often mumbled as if he was talking to someone. Now she knew he was talking to the Ancients.

"Once you left, I was locked out as well. They told me to enjoy my time with the Eagle. I still wonder whether they meant the one I often fly with or the brash young warrior that enriches my life," Broken Spear continued with a smile and a grunt.

In a rare moment of emotion, he had tears in his eyes.

High in the sky above the valley an eagle let out a loud cry.

Broken Spear went on to explain the dangers on the journey North.

The danger will be faced twice, and this danger is once again from a bear," Broken Spear continued.

"This bear will not be talked to. It is the largest bear in existence, and it controls its territory against all trespassers. It is a bear that hunts down its prey and humans are just another animal to hunt," Broken Spear said as he looked at each of the members sitting around.

"I suggested sending thirty of our warriors to accompany you on the journey.

Burly Bear pointed out the logistical problems of having a small army accompany you. So, I suggested sending the most powerful warriors. And here they sit. Here are our team members for the journey to the North," Broken Spear concluded as he pointed to each of the couples sitting around for breakfast.

"Burley Bear, are you and Meadow Flower coming with us," Golden Hawk asked as Broken Spear's message hit home?

"Yes, Quiet Fox has agreed to lead the clan in my absence. Meadow Flower and I are very excited to once again make a journey with the team.

"This is wonderful," both Busy Bee and Quiet Rabbit spoke in unison.

"I am sure with Burley Bear in the lead, even the dangerous bear you have warned us about will see us and give way," Taelo said as he went to Burly Bear and gave him a hug.

He then turned to Sharp Blade and Single Leaf and welcomed them to the team.

Feather-in-the-Wind looked at the new members from the clan of Others that would be coming along on this new journey. She listened as Broken Spear told Taelo that he had wanted more members of the Others on the team. He had seen a battle where Taelo and the team would face a very large number of fighters.

She listened as Taelo thanked Broken Spear but politely declined any more members from the Others.

He joked that he already had eighty wolves to feed and the six Others would eat as much as the eighty wolves.

This meant the team had sixteen members, about eighty wolves and twenty-four mounts. It was the largest team that Taelo had ever taken on a journey.

Feather-in-the-Wind and Running Stag stood and followed Burley Bear as he led the way to a huge circular object covered by a large hide. Saber Scar and Sharp Blade crawled under and raised a pole at its center. The hide went up and nine sleds were now visible.

"Look at each sled. Each is larger than the ones we made before. There is always room for one person to sleep under the sled covering. The sleds hook together to form a tight wall and the hide serving as the roof can be quickly attached to each sled," Burley Bear began the explanation.

"Here is a really exciting feature. The sleds have been matched to travois poles. See the grooves in the poles. The sled runners match the grooves. They can be mounted on the travois and pulled by the mounts," Saber Scar talked rapidly as he and Sharp Blade strapped one of the sleds to the travois poles.

Single Leaf brought in a mount and the travois was attached to a shoulder harness designed for the mount.

"This is amazing. How did you decide on nine sleds," Feather-in-the-Wind asked as she went to each one and took in the intricate work?

"These sleds are larger than the ones you already have so we have designed the wolf harness to have ten wolves per sled. So, we have a wolf army with us." Burley Bear went on to explain.

"Where will we get the food to feed this army," Running Stag inquired?

"Little Otter and Talking Wren send their greetings. They also sent enough dried buffalo meat to fill every sled. That is the stack over in the corner," Burley Bear said as he pointed to stacked bundles of goods wrapped in leather.

"It seems everyone in the three clans has been working together in getting our team ready to travel on this next journey," Taelo said as he took in the team and the equipment.

"Yes, this trip like no other has brought all of us closer together. Broken Spear has spoken with each of the clan leaders and has highlighted how our fortunes have improved with each journey. He says he got his new energy from you. He has challenged all of us to contribute to the continued improvement of the clan," Burley Bear said as he put his arm around Taelo's shoulder.

Feather-in-the-Wind looked at the huge pack of wolves that now surrounded her. They seemed to have chosen her as their leader.

"These sleds tied to the travois provide a really great way to carry all our goods. And even when tied to the travois the circle of sleds can be achieved and the living area established," Running Stag commented. He had learned that it had been Burley Bear that had come up with the ingenious idea of the combination of sled and travois.

Taelo addressed the team after his meeting with Broken Spear. He described the danger of the giant bears. He described the encounter they would have with enemies with eyes the color of the sky.

"We need to get our mounts use to facing both the bear and humans with weapons. I think having Burley Bear act the part of the giant bear would be appropriate," Feather-in-the-Wind said jokingly.

"Yes, I will be the practice bear," Burley Bear said as he let out a roar and pretended to attack Feather-in-the-Wind.

Just then a runner came in with the news that someone was approaching along the coast. He thought it might be from the Elk Clan because there was someone almost the size of Burley Bear riding a mount.

"Ha. He did make it on time," Burley Bear said as he turned to follow the runner out of the cave.

"I see you will have two more members of your team to accompany you," Broken Spear said with a smile.

"Hello, the team," Small Otter called out as he was led to the preparation area by Burley Bear.

"Oh, I am so happy we made it on time," Talking Wren said as she went about greeting everyone.

She was as animated as Feather-in-the-Wind remembered.

The team departed as the sun rose on the following sun cycle.

Feather-in-the-Wind was walking behind the eleven mounts with Walker, Arrow and Lasher and the rest of the wolf pack. It was clear Lasher had asserted his dominance.

Feather-in-the-Wind had again demonstrated her keen ability to have the wolves mind her.

"Would you have imagined such a scene when we waited for the man of the Eagle to guide us," Broken Spear said to Quiet Fox as they stood together watching the departing team?

"How could we have known what a difference he would make on our lives," Quiet Fox replied as he slowly waved a goodbye.

Ahead of Feather-in-the-Wind the twin peaks on the way north to the lodge of the Northern Elk Clan graced the afternoon sky. The sun setting cast its last rays on the snow cap of the Eastern most peak and turned it almost a pure yellow. The edges of the snow cape turned almost black where the dark green of the sentinel pines created its dark skirt.

Feather-in-the-Wind loved this point in all returning trips, she like everyone else on the trail looked forward to stopping to enjoy the bounty of the small lake surrounded by willows and edged by a few cattails and a game wealthy surrounding area.

The abundance of the rabbits, squirrels, other small game and the frog and fish population of the small lake assured the those stopping of a good meal and a comfortable evening stay.

"It is good to see the twin peaks. We will camp here tonight. Tomorrow we will reach the Northern Elk Clan and be greeted by White Feather," Golden Hawk said as their caravan came slowly down the path to the lake.

Feather-in-the-Wind knew that White Swan's new nickname had become White Feather. Her leadership spear was adorned with the feather of a White Swan.

Her position as the only woman clan leader had elevated her to an almost reverent position. She inspired Feather-in-the-Wind and every other young woman in the Elk Clan.

White Swan was not only an inspiration, but she was a model of how to maneuver as a woman in a strong male society.

She listened as Taelo asked Burley Bear to lead the team in setting up their lodge.

Burley Bear moved each of the team members into the position where they belonged. The travois with the sleds mounted on them were easily pulled into position by the mounts. The mounts ended up on the outside of the circle formed by the positioning of the sleds.

The rider of each mount dismounted and together with their partner proceeded to detach the travois from the mount.

It took both persons on each travois to lower the travois to the ground. It was clear that several of the team pairs were not strong enough for this task.

Feather-in-the-Wind and Running Stag basically dropped their travois. She cried out that she needed a stronger partner.

"Let's put this travois back up and then see if we can use the rope to lower it to the ground," Running Stag suggested.

Running Stag tied one end of the rope for the travois onto the mount harness. He then had Saber Scar and Sharp Blade lift the travois up. He secured the travois to the harness.

"Let me show you how to lower the travois by loosening the travois ropes and letting it slide around the travois shaft," Running Stag said to Feather-in-the-Wind.

The two easily lowered the travois.

"Any of us can lower the travois in this manner," Running Stag commented, "raising it up to tie it off is another matter.

"We will need to think about how each of us can raise the travois into place. Either we come up with a way to do it or Saber Scar and Sharp Blade will be very busy each time we get ready to move on," Running Stag pointed out.

Once all the travois were lowered, the mounts were led away to their holding area.

"Good work, we have an almost perfect circle," Little Otter commented as he walked around the inside of the sled circle.

He was tying the sleds together as Burley Bear continued his instructions.

Meadow Flower, Sharp Blade, Single Leaf, Saber Scar and Marigold positioned the ten poles to be used to hold up the outside edges of the cover. These poles went up on the inside perimeter of the sleds.

There was a holding loop the pole would be tied to once it was in place. The top was large enough to cover the sleds and then be tied off at the base of each sled.

This created a completely closed enclosure. A section was cut in such a way as to form a doorway between two sleds. The door could be closed by moving the sled into position so that it connected the first and last sleds.

Meadow Flower placed the longest pole in the center of the circle. She and Saber Scar then positioned and rolled out the hide that made up the cover of their shelter.

"This is the tricky part. One person from each sled must attach their pole to the loop hanging down inside of the cover. The other from that sled must anchor the pole to a stake driven deeply into the ground on the far side of the sled. We must all do this together and at the same time.

One person must stand in the middle and push up the center pole," Meadow Flower said as she got the covering positioned.

"Let me show each of you the loop and how the pole, the loop and the tie off rope must be positioned," Meadow Flower continued her instruction.

"I will be the center," Burley Bear volunteered.

"The strongest person at each sled must be the one pulling the poles up and anchoring it," Burley Bear continued.

"I guess I will let Quiet Rabbit pull up our pole. I know she is the strongest, of the two of us," Taelo joked as he attached the tie line to the top of the pole at his sled.

He was not sure he would be strong enough for this effort.

They were also missing three of their team members. This meant two of the sleds did not have anyone to pull up the poles.

After much straining and with Marigold, Meadow Flower, Saber Scar, Sharp Blade and Single Leaf running around to help each of the other members the cover was up.

It was clear to Taelo that the team did not have the required strength to do this every evening.

"We should use our mounts to pull up the cover for our shelter. Your clan members are at least twice as strong as the rest of us and had no problem, but we are exhausted by this effort," Running Stag said as he sat down. He felt a little dejected. He was not use, to feeling so weak and vulnerable.

"My pole would not have gone up if Marigold had not come over and helped me," Running Stag continued.

He was not strong enough on his own to pull up the weight of the cover.

"Yes, the use of the mount is a great idea and the person inside the circle can tie off the pole," Feather-in-the-Wind added.

"There is enough time. Let's practice that now," she suggested.

Everyone knew that they would indeed try it at least one more time.

"Everyone take a break and maybe have something to eat while Burley Bear and I mark each line, so we know where to put the loop," Taelo announced.

"Running Stag has come up with two good ideas. I hope he figures out how to raise the travois onto the mounts. He is right about the fact that most of the team cannot raise the travois up. Quiet Rabbit and I cannot lift it," Taelo shared with Burley Bear.

"We did not realize how weak you new ones are," Burley Bear said as he gave Taelo a shoulder hug.

He felt bad about having missed the fact that the team would not have the strength to carry out some of these critical tasks.

"How did we miss the idea of using the mounts or on using the rope to lower the travois," Single Leaf said to Sharp Blade as they watched Taelo and Burley Bear marking the lines.

After the ropes had been marked and the team had eaten, Burley Bear had everyone get into position to lower the cover.

Once everyone was in place, the cover was lowered.

It took almost as much effort to lower it as to raise it.

The lowering looked more like an uncontrolled collapse then a lowering.

"I am glad we did this. It was just as hard to take the cover down as it was to put it up. We will want to use the mounts on both occasions," Busy Bee said.

"Let's go get the mounts and put them in position," Meadow Flower said loud enough for the whole team to hear.

"This time it was really easy. Let's take it down and do it again," Little Otter joked as the covering went smoothly up.

"That is a great idea," Running Stag said.

"I was just joking," Little Otter replied with a verbal groan.

But the rest of the team agreed with Running Stag.

"It really did get easier," Talking Wren commented as the covering came up for the third time."

Suddenly, Feather-in-the-Wind jumped up and ran out of the compound.

"I don't know where she is going or what she is doing. I will go see if I can be of help," Running Stag commented as he got up.

"I will go with you," Single Leaf said as she followed Running Stag out.

A short time later Feather-in-the-Wind, Running Stag and Single Leaf returned.

Feather-in-the-Wind was carrying two stout but slender poles about the height of her shoulders that were tied close to one end. She spread the two poles and a small V formed at the top.

Single Leaf lowered the pole she was carrying into the V. This pole was about the thickness of Taelo's forearm.

Running Stag also had two stout poles that were tied in the middle and opened to make an X.

The three walked over to Feather-in-the-Wind's sled.

Single Leaf set up the tall poles with the V at the top at about the middle of the distance between the sled and the end of the travois.

Feather-in-the-Wind put the thick pole into the V and the end under the front cross member of the travois.

Running Stag had his X opened and in position between the main pole that would do the raising and the travois cross member.

Single Leaf held the main lever pole and the pivot point.

Feather-in-the-Wind reached up to grasp the end of the pole. It was at the limit of her reach. She pulled down on the pole and the travois came smoothly up.

When it was high enough, Running Stag put the X frame under the main travois cross members. It had a slight lean toward the back of the travois.

The three then stepped back and the travois stayed in the raised position.

"We demonstrated this with three people but the three of us have already figured out how one person can do it," Feather-in-the-Wind proudly shared the procedure she had thought up.

"I am so impressed that I have grilled each of you a choice piece of meat," Little Otter said as he brought each of them a seasoned and grilled piece of meat.

"I will help you finish your design and get it ready for each of the travois," Meadow Flower volunteered.

Feather-in-the-Wind basked in the praise everyone gave to her and to Running Stag. Together they had solved the major problems of how the team was going to handle their sled loaded travois and how to raise and lower their enclosure.

She had been challenged by Running Stag's innovative mind and had not wanted to be out done. Her breakthrough in how to lift the heavy load came from her memory of watching the stone masons of her village moving and lifting the large stones into position. She was impressed in how quickly Running Stag caught on. He had contributed the idea of the X brace to hold the travois poles in place after they were lifted.

That evening as they went to sleep, she gave him a hug and whispered that she thought him to be very smart. He replied that of course he was as corroborated by who was sleeping next to him.

Feather-in-the-Wind was one of the last to rise. Bold Walker had finally started to lick her cheek in concern.

"Here, I think I am waking to an eager mate and find myself looking into the eyes of a wolf," she mumbled as she wiped off her face.

Running Stag brought over a bowl of stew and sat down beside her.

He touched her cheek and just smiled. He knew better than to say anything.

Taelo called for the cover to be brought down. The team rallied and together utilizing the mounts the covering came down smoothly.

Taelo praised everyone for the smooth execution. He was very pleased with how well they had lowered and stored the covering.

Feather-in-the-Wind, Single leaf and Running Stag supervised each team in lifting and attaching the travois to the mounts.

Little Otter volunteered to make a lifting rig for each of the travois.

"Congratulation, we seem to have mastered setting up and taking down our camp," Taelo commented as the team made ready to leave.

Let's plan on setting up our camp in the open yard outside of the lodge. Let's show the Northern Elk Clan our new capability and the grand gift from Burley Bear, Meadow Flower and the rest of the Others," Taelo said as the team readied to leave the lake.

A few hours later they crossed the river and started up the tributary leading to the Northern Elk Clan lodge.

Taelo and Golden Hawk rode side by side with their golden feathers hanging from their upright spears.

Feather-in-the-Wind was last with eighty wolves surrounding her.

The team with its eighteen mounts, eleven travois and an eighty-member wolfpack following behind them made a formidable sight.

"You left on four mounts with three wolves. You return with a full clan behind you," White Swan said as she gave both Taelo and Golden Hawk a hug.

"And the two of you look as strong as ever," she continued as she hugged Burley Bear and Meadow Flower.

"I know from all the stories and our brief meeting that you are Saber Scar and Marigold," White Swan continued down the line giving her hugs.

"It eases my mind when two more of you join the team. I know now this team is equipped for all problems," White Swan said when greeting Sharp Blade and Single Leaf.

"And here is the famous Talking Wren and her Little Otter. I had no idea you would be joining. How is Red Oak and Quiet Pheasant," White Swan continued her greetings.

"It is always good to have all my daughters return safely.

I see my youngest has returned once again as the wolf woman," White Swan continued her greeting and comments as she gave each of the three a hug.

She had purposely called them all her daughters signaling a status elevation to the rest of the clan.

"I am honored to be your "youngest" daughter. I want my "older sisters" to take note," Feather-in-the-Wind said as she winked at Quiet Rabbit and Busy Bee.

"Now I know why I love to be with this team so much," Feather-in-the-Wind thought to herself. She had just been rewarded by being called a daughter.

She and the team put up a demonstration of raising their lodge in the green area to the side of the Elk Clan's lodge.

Chapter 13:

"It's time to go. The wolves are going to eat all their food before we even begin the journey," Feather-in-the-Wind announced a few evenings later after coming back in from feeding them.

"Tomorrow we organize and check all our gear. We have a good supply of everything we can think of needing," Taelo said from the log he was sitting on.

The next morning Feather-in-the-Wind heard Taelo making a comment about leaving but he needed to get a half a block of salt. She was surprised when he also asked permission for the team to spend a night at the cave where the Elk Clan had first established themselves and then begin their journey from there.

"May we accompany you and spend the night with you at the cave," White Swan inquired?

"It is I who is asking for permission to use the council chambers. Of course, you are welcome and perhaps you and Grey Fox Running could tell the stories of old. Quiet Rabbit, Busy Bee, Meadow Flower, Feather-in-the-Wind and Marigold would like to put up drawings of, the team hunt, the *Journey to the land of the Condor* and the *Journey of Discovery*. They are eager to share them with you to get your approval," Taelo replied.

White Feather replied that she loved the idea of such an evening.

Feather-in-the-Wind was surprised to hear her name, but it was an honor to be included in the group that would put drawings up on the wall.

The word, about the team's departure, traveled quickly through the entire clan living area. By the time the mounts were led into the compound the entire clan had gathered to watch.

High in the sky an eagle circled and let out a cry.

The team headed up the valley.

Feather-in-the-Wind rode her mount. Bold Walker trotted along beside her. Running Stag and Arrow were to the other side. Running Stag's parents had been invited and followed on their mounts.

She stood on her mount and waved to all the Northern Elk Clan.

A short time later, she entered the cave. The huge chamber shimmered as the sunlight streamed through the blue green translucent cascade of water. The air pulled from the far back opening dispersed as the cave widened and lightly grazed the backs of those sitting and facing the speaker who was standing with his back to the falls.

The sun's rays from the western settling sun cast shimmering rays that flickered in rhythm with the falling waters and the misting spray of countless volumes of water racing to reach the pool at the cliff's base.

Gray Fox Running took in the faces of the Elk Clan and of the Others, all eager to hear stories he had told to many of them in their younger years. He had heard the stories from his father, mother, and grandparents. These were ancient stories about the beginning of the first Elk Clan.

He watched as Quiet Rabbit, Busy Bee, Feather-in-the-Wind, Meadow Flower and Marigold began sketching in the scenes for new drawings being added to the ancient drawings placed there so long ago.

It was a magical meeting of the ghosts of long ago and the spirit and energy of those in the here and now. Gray Fox Running could see the ancients in the flickering light beams streaming over his shoulders as the sun illuminated the cave just before going down behind the mountain to the west.

Soon the flickering of the fire and the glow of the torches was the only separation between the two periods of time. Time came much closer together and a hush came over the gathering.

All the team put their sitting hides around in a semi-circle facing the falls. The leader's circle was immediately in front of them. They all felt the mystical nature of the chamber. They were sitting among the ancients.

Grey Fox Running stopped for a break in the story telling. The new sketches on the wall were taking shape. He walked over and looked at the new sketches and then took a torch to look at the old sketches and the stories they displayed.

"This is my first time to come into the Elk Clan's council chambers. It is amazing," Floating Cloud commented quietly.

"Oh, let's give everyone a quick tour of the chamber and Busy Bee will hang the hides with the scenes we will put on the chamber wall," Quiet Rabbit replied.

After the quick tour, everyone took a helping of food and drink placed near at hand. They were ready for the next story.

Grey Fox Running ended the evening with the story of the Salt Gatherers.

During the story telling, Quiet Rabbit, Busy Bee, Feather-in-the-Wind, Marigold and Meadow Flower were quietly drawing images on the cave wall.

"We are not done but you can see the scenes taking shape," Quite Rabbit said as the story telling ended.

"We will finish the drawings on our return from our travels to the North," Busy Bee continued.

The next morning the team cleaned the council chambers, then they broke camp. By the time the sun was beginning its departure from its eastern mountain tops the team was organized and ready to proceed.

Last night we heard the story of the Elk Clan's arrival. We will be back tracking their journey. Let's hope the same passage is still open," Taelo commented.

I hope the warm weather follows us as we travel," Burley Bear said to Little Otter walking beside him.

"At least we won't be jogging for most of this journey," Little Otter replied.

"Wait until the wolves are pulling our sleds. Then we will all get our turn running," Feather-in-the-Wind said from where she rode her mount.

She remembered the beginning of their *Journey of Discovery*. She had run as much then as when the team had returned from the *Journey to the Condor Clan*. Jogging and running was something this team was always doing.

The team were surprised by the abundance of small game. They had also come across the tracks of larger animals as well.

They set a constant and steady cadence of traveling from sunrise to setting sun. Their morning and high sun meals were eaten on the go.

Their evening meals were taken after camp had been setup.

They carried enough poles to make fish traps along the streams where they stopped. Once the camp was setup the fish traps were put in place. Two of the team would clean the captured fish, rub them with salt, and roast them on the coals of the evening fire. Usually, the hot fish were snacks for the team members but most of the fish were held for the morning meal.

One member of the team always helped Feather-in-the-Wind feed each of the wolves. The wolves were fed the minimum possible. This made them hungry enough to hunt for themselves. Feather-in-the-Wind made sure all the younger wolves got enough eat.

There were two new pups that she at first carried as they traveled. Later they followed Feather-in-the-Wind as much as their natural mother.

"Well team it seems we have figured out how to handle all the routine daily work. The work seems to be well balanced. It is time we began to practice our personal and camp defense," Taelo said to the team.

"Oh, and we will practice each at least three times," Little Otter and Burley Bear said in unison.

The entire team echoed what had been said.

He began and continued to exercise the team in their self-defense practice, He assigned Feather-in-the-Wind to call for a practice at random times, three times each cycle of the sun.

A cycle after Taelo's return from his scouting, the team faced its first challenge.

136

"There is something wrong. The wolves are acting as if they are ready for a fight," Feather-in-the-Wind called out from where she was walking with the wolves. The two young wolves were close on her heals. She picked them up and put them in a sling she had made for them.

"My mount is also nervous," Single Leaf called in reply.

"Feather-in-the-Wind let me know when the wolves gather tight around you," Taelo called back to her.

"How tight do they need to be," Feather-in-the-Wind said as she looked at the pack surrounding her.

"Lasher, go to Feather-in-the-Wind," Taelo said.

Lasher immediately turned and went back to the wolf pack and Feather-in-the-Wind.

Lasher was on one side and Bold Walker was on the other. The two were ready to defend her.

"Feather-in-the-Wind bring the wolves in closer. Bring them into the center when we go into our defensive circle," Taelo called back.

As the sun reached its zenith, Burlcy Bear called for a defensive circle and indicated the area around him as the location for the circle.

Meadow Flower had the lead mount and immediately circled around him. She set the distance with Burley Bear at the center and traveled around until the last two travois where in front of her.

Feather-in-the-Wind rushed through with the wolves following behind. Meadow Flower then turned her mount to the inside of the circle. Each of those following closed the gaps as they in turn put their mounts to the inside.

The circle closed. They had missed perfection by three hand lengths.

"There is a very nice stream and lake ahead. If we move now, we can easily make it before the sun sets," Golden Hawk said as he finished his meal after his return from his scouting trip.

"Let's move," Feather-in-the-Wind said from the middle of the wolf pack that lay around her. She had quickly eaten her lunch snack and had been playing with the two wolf pups. Their mother was peacefully sleeping next to where Feather-in-the-Wind sat.

"I see that you are the safest one among us," Golden Hawk said as he took in the sight of Feather-in-the-Wind surrounded by the team's eighty wolves.

The wolves were sitting looking outward as if in guard duty formation.

"All you have to do is feed them and they love you," she replied with a nod and a smile.

As she stood up the wolves all stood up. It was clear that they saw her as their leader.

The team traveled on in full alert. The mounts were nervous, and the wolves kept close to Feather-in-the-Wind.

Lasher and Walker continued to walk at her side.

"I see you assigned Lasher to guard Feather-in-the-Wind. Do you expect trouble," Golden Hawk asked Taelo?

"Something has the mounts and the wolves on edge.

I am not sure what it is, but Feather-in-the-Wind is behind the team by herself.

Lasher is my insurance of her safety," Taelo replied.

Golden Hawk rode out and picked the position for the camp. The circle was once again made but this time the mounts were to the outer side.

The circle did not close. There was an open section.

This subtle difference caused Taelo to realize that the normal camping circle needed a smaller distance around the center.

The defensive circle needed to have a greater distance around the center. This allowed the front of the travois and the mount to fit in comfortably.

"We were lucky the first time because Meadow Flower instinctively picked the right distance for the defensive circle," Taelo commented.

"This time we have almost the same distance, but we have an open area. We need a tighter circle when the mounts are to the outside.

Let's try it again," Taelo requested.

The team practiced both the defensive circle and the normal camping circle three times.

"I believe I have the distance for each one," Meadow Flower commented after the third try.

"Yes, you do. Tomorrow I would like to have Busy Bee try her hand at setting the defensive circle and the evening circle," Taelo replied.

"We will each take a turn at setting the distance for each circle," Taelo continued.

He wanted the entire team to have this capability.

The team finished setting up camp. They had dinner and then each went to their assigned duties.

"The mounts are nervous. Let's get them together and into the compound," Talking Wren said to Single Leaf immediately after the mounts started to pull on their holding lines.

"Single Leaf is leading the mounts toward the compound," Lily said as she saw the mounts coming toward her.

"Let's move the sled to let her in," Burley Bear said as he quickly jumped up and went to the entrance sled.

He was joined with Meadow Flower and the two moved the sled and travois.

Feather-in-the-Wind and Running Stag were out with the wolves.

"Let's slowly walk back toward the camp," Feather-in-the-Wind said as she picked up the two young wolves and put them in her carrying sling.

"What's wrong," Running Stag asked as he followed Feather-in-the-Wind?

"Lasher and Walker have started to growl, and the hair is standing up straight on their necks," Feather-in-the-Wind replied.

"Arrow is doing the same thing," was Running Stag's reply.

When the camp was in sight and she saw the mounts going into the camp Feather-in-the-Wind said, "Run." She turned and sprinted toward the compound.

"Keep the camp open. Feather-in-the-Wind and our wolves are on the run toward us," Taelo said as Burly Bear, Saber Scar, Little Otter and Golden Hawk stood with their spears to either side of the opening.

"Dire wolves," Feather-in-the-Wind said as she led her wolves into the center and stopped.

She sat down and let the two wolf pups out. The pups went to their mother and snuggled in close to her.

"And that is why no one ever confronts Burley Bear. Two of us can barely move our travois and he does it by himself," Running Stag said quietly to Feather-in-the-Wind as he pointed to Burley Bear.

"Yes, his superior strength is unquestionable. What is even better is that he has grown in wisdom and in leadership through his friendship and devotion to Taelo and Golden Hawk. The three of them are like brothers. They are connected," Feather-in-the-Wind replied.

"I suppose that is why Burley Bear chose to come on this journey. It makes me feel much safer to have him with us," Running Stag continued as he drew the covering over the two of them.

The following morning Taelo put her up front with all her wolves.

His instructions were simple, "Feather-in-the-Wind, please lead the way with your wolves. Watch Lasher and Walker. Let me know if either of them growls or has the hair on the back of their neck standing on end."

"I guess we are the dire wolf food," Little Otter joked as he and Burley Bear passed by Feather-in-the-Wind to take the lead for the team.

"Good that means they will be full by the time they get to me and won't be hungry," Feather-in-the-Wind joked back.

Later, Taelo and Golden Hawk took the lead and jogged out in front of the entire procession. Their slings seemed to be in continuous use. Lasher was now up front with Taelo and would go out and retrieve the game and bring it to either Taelo or Golden Hawk.

"Hey, give us a chance," Running Stag called out as he watched the two in action.

"You will be up here tomorrow, and we will expect you to do the same," Taelo responded.

"Any other comments," Talking Wren said from the other side of the mounts from Running Stag.

Feather-in-the-Wind and the rest of the team traveled for more than a moon cycle. Taelo kept the team active and practiced. She took note of how he kept the work balanced. Everyone was assigned for some period to every task and role. She and Running Stag spent the most time with the wolves. Quiet Rabbit, Busy Bee, and Talking Wren spent the most time with the mounts. Lily and Floating Cloud were the normal cooks, but everyone took a turn with one of them.

Feather-in-the-wind saw Quiet Rabbit and Busy Bee returning from their scouting trip.

She watched as Lily grilled two pieces of fresh meat on the fire

Feather-in-the-wind heard Quiet Rabbit describe the passage ahead as beautiful and inspiring as seeing the sun rise on one sea and set on the other as they had witnessed on their journey to the land of the Condor.

Feather-in-the-Wind decided that someday she too would go and see that sight that was on the way to the land of her birth.

The team proceeded ahead. Feather-in-the-Wind and Running Stag alternated in riding their mounts and guiding the wolf pulled sled.

She was looking forward to the passage that Quiet Rabbit had described. She was also fascinated by the wavering green lights that entertained them each evening.

So far, the journey had been very relaxing and enjoyable.

Chapter 14:

The mountains continued to grow in size, height and snow covering. It seemed to Feather-in-the-Wind that the team had traveled toward the towering peaks for the last moon cycle and made little progress. In fact, the size of the mountains, were so overwhelming that the eye played a trick on the mind. Now the team was within the grasp of the mountain's afternoon and evening shadows and the team's small and fragile existence was exposed.

Feather-in-the-Wind looked at the flat stone, with a large round one on top of the flat stone and then a small round one next to it to indicate the direction to follow.

She pointed the marker out and then pointed to the next one she could see from her perch on top of her mount. She then urged her mount forward and hurried to find the next marker.

She was just about to move on when Lasher appeared and went to Quiet Rabbit. She was at first concerned but Quiet Rabbit commented that Lasher was behaving in the manner he did when he was told to go to a particular person. She was sure because he sat down quietly at her feet.

She rode forward and spotted the location Taelo had marked for the camp. Just beyond it she could see the small river. On a large bush she spotted the large fish hanging and knew that Golden Hawk and Taelo had left the team a fish large enough to feed all of them. The bag of rabbits and one squirrel she had hanging from her waist would round out the meal.

"This is the spot. They left a gift for us," Lily called out as she spotted the fish hanging on a pole at the edge of the riverbank.

"Let's set up camp and this time we will put the cover up as well. The weather is getting colder each evening," Busy Bee called out. It was her turn to lead the setup.

Feather-in-the-Wind dismounted and stood at the center of what would be the teams camp. She waited as Busy Bee guided the team in a circle and called for the cover to be raised.

The waters of the lake in the sky lay above and ahead of them. Directly above them cutting through the top of the mountain was a thin blue river. An almost straight vertical blue line brought the thin blue river down from above to the waters that gathered from a gently flowing river into the waters that shot forcefully through the narrow gorge.

Feather-in-the-Wind absorbed the three-dimensional visual game her eyes played with the sky, the mountain cliffs and the river gorge as morning changed the gash from black to a brilliant blue.

She watched and listened as Taelo, and Golden Hawk returned and explained how they planned to get the team up through the waters spewing out of the gorge formed by the cliffs.

She laughed when Burley Bear and Saber Scar both realized and commented that they were strong, but they would need all the pulling help possible to get the first mount pulled up to the upstream beach. She went up to both and gave them a reassuring hug and volunteered to help pull.

Since she was the smallest and probably the weakest, the entire team laughed.

Talking Wren accepted Taelo's request to organize and guide the team's passage through the river gorge.

Feather-in-the-Wind was impressed by Talking Wren's ability to think through all that would be required to get the team through.

She volunteered to gather the materials and construct the platform that would hold the wolves on their trip through the gorge.

She, Quiet Rabbit, and Running Stag spent an entire sun cycle weaving the platform floor.

The next sun cycle she participated in getting all the team's possessions in the order they would be pulled across. She organized the wolves at the rear. They would be the last to go through the gap.

She and Running Stag got the task of placing the cross member that went across the chest of the floating mount. She watched as Quiet Rabbit and Busy Bee placed a similar cross member across the rear of the mount. This effectively locked the mount into its floating carrier and made it ready to be pulled through the gap.

When Golden Hawk stumbled out of the water on legs that he could barely stand on, Feather-in-the-Wind knew that there was a major problem. The mount would have the same problem as it got pulled through the gorge. Its legs would be numb, and it would not be able to stand.

She followed Quiet Rabbit and Busy Bee through the gorge as they crossed to the other side on the narrow trail.

The mount made it to the point where it was shallow enough for it to stand but it was clear its legs were not functioning properly.

She rushed forward and placed a cover over the mounts head. This would keep it from panicking.

She was in the ice cold water and realized just how cold it was.

Running Stag loosened the back member so the frame could be pulled away from the mount.

She held the mounts head out of the water as the rest of the team pulled the mount to the beach.

"Thank you for holding her head. Your wolves are wondering where you went. And Nudge is the mount Floating Cloud and I share," Bashful Lark said as she talked quietly to her mount.

It was clear the mount recognized Bashful Lark's voice. It let out a snort and gave Bashful Lark a nudge.

"I think I know how you named her," Feather-in-the-Wind said as she signaled Running Stag and headed back to the gap.

It three sun cycles later it was finally the time to get all the wolves through.

She got up on the platform and called for the wolves to join her. About a third of the wolves responded to her call. That made a full load, but it was clear to her that some of the wolves would need extra encouragement to get on the floating platform. She shouted, "stay", at a couple of the wolves that were going to leap for the platform as it was pulled up stream.

"You have trained them well. I will want to enroll you in helping me handle any bears we run into," Taelo said as he thought about the confrontation that had been predicted.

"Thank you for your praise. Let me know what I can do to help," Feather-in-the-Wind said looking up from where she sat with the wolves around her.

Her emotions spiked as she realized Taelo had praised her and asked for her help.

It took four pulls to get all the wolves through the gap. Lasher proved to be the driver as the last of the reluctant wolves were being loaded. He growled and nipped at their heels and back sides of the wolves that were hesitant.

"They may see you as their human leader, but it is clear that Lasher is their wolf master. They dare not ignore him," Taelo commented to Feather-in-the-Wind as they got the last of the wolves on the platform.

"Slow Runner, Sharp Blade and I will clean up this area and then come up to the beach," Running Stag called out as the last pull began the journey through the gap.

Feather in the Wind waved at him and shouted that she would be waiting.

The team camp was setup just north of the landing beach. The mounts were tethered by the river and the wolves were situated on the mountain side of the camp.

Taelo approached her about being his partner in fighting any bear that might attack the team. She was honored to be singled out. It turned out her ability to handle the wolf pack played a major role on how Taelo planned to respond to a bear attack.

He planned to attract the bear to chase him. He then wanted her to bring her wolf army up behind the bear and harass it. He would then see if the bear could be driven off. If not, then he would kill it.

She did not know what to expect but she knew she would do whatever was asked.

In the last bear encounter she had climbed high up a pine tree and had watched as Taelo fearlessly faced a huge bear. He had killed it even as the bear grasped him in its clutches. The bear almost took Taelo's life when its claws dug deep through Taelo's back.

Running Stag volunteered to help but Taelo pointed out that only she was being asked and that everyone else had a role. The role was to get the team away from the bear.

Quiet Rabbit sat quietly. She could run as fast, and she had volunteered just as eagerly as Running Stag.

"We need you to be ready to sew us up if we need it," Taelo had quietly replied as he gave her a hug.

He loudly made the point that he was only asking the help of Feather-in-the-Wind so the rest of the team would hear.

"You know all of us are having a hard time accepting the role of running instead of fighting together," Golden Hawk spoke up.

He, Busy Bee, Quiet Rabbit and Taelo had discussed and argued this during their night on the river beach.

The actions Taelo was asking the team to accept were foreign to all of them. The team culture was one of coming together to overcome any obstacle.

"Yes, we will be acting as a team. In the past as a team, we were the superior power. In this case we are not. We will be the hunted. But we are smarter than the hunter.

The team will win the battle because we choose to fight on our terms not on the bear's term.

"Feather-in-the-Wind and her wolves will be my army. We will hound and tire the bear to exhaustion and then we will return to the team.

I hope in this manner to keep the team moving safely in the direction we desire to go," Taelo replied.

"I at least will volunteer to be the bear for our practices," Burley Bear spoke and broke the silence that had followed Taelo's comments.

"And so, will I," Little Otter said as he put his arm around Burley Bear.

"Great idea to practice," Taelo replied.

For once he had not thought about the practice.

As always, they practiced three times.

"Is Taelo always this thorough," Slow Runner asked?

"Yes, and it has served the team well. We all groan while we are doing what he asks and then we are rejoicing when the practice saves us," Running Stag replied.

"If we are in camp when we face the bear, let Feather-in-the-Wind and I draw the bear away, then abandon the camp and ride your mounts away in the same manner." Taelo commented as the team ate their evening meal.

"You and the wolves did a superb job at chasing Burley Bear. You should stay away as far as possible. The bear may not run away but instead attack. In that case you turn and run.

I will then get the bear's attention and make him chase me. When he does, you must again have the wolves chase the bear. We will do this until we tire out the bear," Taelo sat discussing his strategy on how to handle an attacking bear.

"I understand and you can count on me and the wolves," Feather-in-the-Wind replied.

It was on the seventh sun cycle after the team had just broken camp that they ran into the bear. It came roaring out from a depression that was behind a large boulder.

"Go," Sharp Blade said as he hit the mount Single Leaf was riding.

This single action saved her and the mount. The bear knocked the sled and travois sideways. Single Leaf urged her mount forward and the travois came clear of the bear.

Sharp Blade turned and ran back toward the pack of wolves.

"Attack," Feather-in-the-Wind said as she fearlessly ran forward with her wolves.

The wolves were no match for the huge beast.

Taelo turned and ran back from the front of the procession. He had his spear out and was yelling at the top of his voice.

"Feather-in-the-Wind let's do what we said," Taelo called out as he attracted the bear.

Suddenly the bear focused on Taelo.

The chase was on.

"Come on you slow beast," Taelo called over his shoulder.

"This bear is much faster than I thought," went through Taelo's mind a few moments later.

Taelo could hear Feather-in-the-Wind urging her wolves on as they followed on the heel of the great bear.

The bear was ignoring the wolves and was focused on Taelo.

Suddenly it stopped and turned.

"It's after me," Feather-in-the-Wind called out as she turned and ran.

Wolves flew in both directions as the bear pawed aside the wolves who were trying to protect Feather-in-the-Wind.

Taelo turned and ran after the bear from behind.

His dream was coming to life. He knew that in the next few moments what he had seen in his delusional dreams, during the recovery from his wounds, would come true. He had lived this experience once before. Now he knew the dream had been about this bear not the one that had attacked him then.

"Your skin will be my bed. Your claws will be my blade. Your meat will feed my body. You will die today," Taelo called out as he caught up with the bear and buried his spear into the side of the bear.

The bear gave a giant roar and stood on his hind legs and turned on Taelo.

Taelo ran toward the bear and at the last moment slid past him on the ground. As he went sliding past the bear, his blade cut across the back of the bear's leg just above the paws.

The bear tried to turn but slowly lost its balance and toppled over. As it got on its other three legs, Taelo cut the tendon in the other back leg.

Feather-in-the-Wind had her wolves gathered around her. She ran back toward the bear with her spear and then retreated as the bear lunged toward her.

"Thank you. See if you can distract the bear so, I can attack it with my war club," Taelo called out.

"My pleasure," Feather-in-the-Wind called out as she teased the Bear with her spear.

Taelo approached the bear from the back. He stepped on the bear's hind quarter and propelled himself in a lunge that allowed him to deliver a solid blow to the side of the bear's head just below its ear.

The crack and crunch signaled significant damage.

The loud roar and the sudden lunge toward Taelo made it clear the bear was not through.

"Hiiii eee," Feather-in-the-Wind cried out as she ran forward with all her speed and buried the spear in the bear's left side just below the front leg.

The bear swiped at her with its right paw.

Feather-in-the-Wind went sliding past the bear and immediately ran past Taelo.

"He is all yours," she said as she went past.

"I will thank you later," Taelo said as he hit the bear on the other side of its head with his war club and spun away.

The bear went down with a grunt. He was stunned but not yet dead.

Taelo jumped on its back and with a small hand weapon made of shark teeth bound between two elk jaw bones, he cut the bear's throat. He then hit it on the back of its head with all his might.

The bear was finally dead.

As he turned to share the news with Feather-in-the-Wind, Taelo saw that she was lying on the ground surrounded by her wolves.

Lasher was at her side.

"Where are you wounded," Taelo asked as he rushed to where Feather-in-the-Wind was lying?

"I think the bear cut me across my thigh," was her faint reply.

She had rushed past the bear and had not felt the claw cut across her inner thigh. When she stopped she had been surprised by the blood running down her leg. She knew then that she was seriously hurt.

Taelo quickly examined the wound. It was bleeding in a pulsing fashion. He pulled his medicine bag from his belt and took out a piece of leather and some gum material.

"This may sting," Taelo said as he wiped the wound clean, put the gum material into the wound and bound it in tight with a wide leather strap.

"Go to Quiet Rabbit," Taelo said as he patted Lasher on the head.

Lasher ran off circled the area once and then chose a direction toward the camp.

Taelo succeeded in stopping the flow of blood from the wound in Feather-in-the-Wind's thigh. It was clear to him she had lost a lot of blood.

Her wolves were lying on the ground around her. Taelo looked around and counted three dead wolves. Several were wounded but with some care they would survive.

Feather-in-the-Wind came awake, but she felt faint and very weak and said nothing but closed her eyes when she saw Quiet Rabbit examining her wound.

She heard Taelo as he praised her.

Feather-in-the-Wind is fearless. She is swift and she uses her size to the fullest. She is a giant in her bravery. She was the reason I was able to get the better of this bear," Taelo commented as he helped with the skinning of the bear.

"Let's hope she recovers fully from this attack. I know that Running Stag is worried," Lily commented as she skillfully separated the bear hide from the flesh.

"Yes, those two have the same relationship that Quiet Rabbit and I have with each other. We have all found mates with matching spirits. Together we are one. Apart we are less," Taelo said as he thought about the other members of the team.

"In fact, when you think about it, it seems that all our team members have the same close relationship with their mates," Golden Hawk replied.

"You're right, it seems very clear once you point this out. We have a team that embraces each other and have similar values. That is probably why we function so well," Lily offered.

"Put Feather-in-the-Wind close to the fire. Put up a wind break around her so the heat is trapped and will warm her," Quiet Rabbit instructed.

"Here is some hot broth for her to drink," Floating Cloud said as she put the bowl to Feather-in-the-Wind's lips.

When he returned to the camp, Taelo inquired, "How is she doing?"

Lasher went up to Feather-in-the-Wind and lay down beside her. Bold Walker was resting on the other side.

"She lost a lot of blood. She will be weak for several moon cycles," Quiet Rabbit replied.

"She had a little broth but now she seems to be sleeping. I think she will be fine by the morning. She will be warm here by the fire.

Lily, I and Floating Cloud will stay by her side tonight," Busy Bee added.

"It has been quite a long time since Taelo has been this worried," Quiet Rabbit said.

"I hope it was not my fault," Feather-in-the-Wind spoke up quietly. She had come around and had been listening with her eyes closed.

"No, it is that we will be in bear territory for a long time. If they all act as this one did, we will be in for many encounters. He is worried about our ability to outwit them," Quiet Rabbit replied.

"It is good to see that you are awake and feeling better," Taelo said on the next sunrise as he and Golden Hawk walked along the line of travois in their inspection routine.

"We are short one wolf pack leader.

I have recruited Golden Hawk as my partner if we meet another bear. These animals are not only huge and aggressive but as you and I learned, they are fast, have endurance and in close combat they are agile," Taelo commented to Feather-in-the-Wind.

"Yes, a little faster than I expected," Feather-in-the-Wind commented.

The conversation allowed Taelo to let the rest of the team know how they would respond to the next bear.

"We are going to try distraction if we meet another of these animals. From what this animal had in its stomach it is clear they eat anything they find.

Golden Hawk and I have prepared pieces of meat and bundles of fruit. Perhaps we can distract them when they approach.

If they pursue us, we will pelt them with shards of stone from our slings.

Finally, we have decided to use our spears as we do when we run down the buffalo but in this case we will wait until the bear is charging us and then plant the butt of our spear in the ground and let the bear run itself onto the spear," Taelo continued his explanation.

On the fourth day a caribou crossed their path in hasty flight from some unseen enemy.

"The wolves are growling," Lily called out from the back of the procession.

"Prepare to execute our plan," Golden Hawk called out as his mount nervously went forward.

Out of a small depression a giant bear charged toward Taelo.

His mount reared up and fell over backwards.

Taelo pushed off and to the side, but he landed directly in front of the path of the bear.

The mount recovered and made its retreat away from the bear.

Suddenly the bear stopped in its track as the shards of stone cut into its snout.

The roar that followed made it clear it was now in a frenzied crazed state.

"Let's run like the wind," Golden Hawk said as he pulled Taelo to his feet.

"I am with you," Taelo replied as he and Golden Hawk led the bear away from the team.

The bear took in all the movement around him and hesitated for a moment.

Suddenly he was hit again by shards of stone. This sealed his direction. He took off at full speed after the two figures in front of him.

"Golden Hawk just rescued Taelo from the bear," Feather-in-the-Wind called out from where she was sitting on the travois. She was still recovering from her wounds and was not yet ready to ride her mount.

"They are now running like the wind and the bear is keeping up," she continued her narrative as the team made its escape in the opposite direction.

"Tell us what you did to that poor bear. We heard its mighty roar." Quiet Rabbit asked after she had given Taelo a hug when he returned.

"Well, Golden Hawk was running so slow that I knew he would get caught at any moment. Lasher and his pack were just too slow to catch up. So, I turned and ran back to the bear and told him to stop being a bully. That roar you heard was after I slapped him a few times for talking back to me," Taelo said in a serious voice.

Burley Bear started laughing.

"You should leave the story telling to Little Otter and me. After all, around you good story telling is the only thing we have left to call our own," Burley Bear said as he stood up and gave Taelo a hug.

"Now tell us the real story," Busy Bee said to Golden Hawk.

Golden Hawk told the team how he and Taelo who were both running at their top speed were slowly being overtaken by the bear. Lasher and the wolf pack attacked, and the bear stopped his pursuit of them. This gave me and Taelo the chance to turn and use our slings to hit the bear in the face and eyes with stone shards.

The bear was not killed but he was badly wounded, and it stopped the pursuit. He, Taelo and the wolves were able to get back to the team.

Golden Hawk walked over and gave Lasher a piece of meat and thanked him for attacking at just the right moment.

"I hope we clear the territory of these bears soon. They are huge and faster and meaner than they look," Feather-in-the-Wind said.

She was finally able to walk around on her own after more than half a moon cycle of recovery.

Chapter 15:

It was hard for Feather-in-the-Wind to distinguish individual animals in the mass stretching out as far as the eye could see. The brown undulating surface stretched to the horizon in all directions. The ground appeared to be brown and seemed alive as the herd moved slowly toward the northeast.

She noted that closer to the team, individual animals stood out and she could see the low head at the end of a short downward sloping neck. Thick horns came out the sides of the head and curved back toward each other. This buffalo was shorter and broader than the ones back in the Elk Clan territory, but it was a powerful looking animal.

The hair on its hide was longer and gave the animal an appearance of floating as it moved slowly along.

Their presence was a welcome sight. The team would be able hunt and be well prepared for the coming cold.

The team had as usual set up their lodge and their camp were totally functional. Floating Cloud and Lily were tending the fire and would have a meal ready for the team on its return from their first hunt. The team never left one person to be on their own. There were just too many problems that could come up.

Feather-in-the-Wind agreed with Busy Bee on the similarities of these animals to the buffalo they were familiar with.

"They seem a little shorter, but they are huge," Talking Wren continued the observation.

"The herd is huge. I am not sure I can see across it," Slow Runner added.

"It is good we stopped and made camp. The herd is slowly making its way across our intended travel path. Perhaps by morning it will be clear of our route," Quiet Rabbit said from where she sat on a large boulder.

Running Stag wondered if the team needed to replenish their meat supply.

"Yes, we should do that. The wolves eat a huge amount of meat. We should get at least one of these beasts to make sure we have enough," Feather-in-the-Wind replied.

The view of the herd was mesmerizing. She watched as Taelo, Quiet Rabbit, Golden Hawk and Busy Bee went out together to take down the first buffalo. Taelo had promised that each hunt team would get a chance to take down a buffalo as well.

The team had made it through the mountain pass but now the days were getting colder and soon winter would be upon them. Their food supply was good but with eighty wolves needing to be fed they went through a great amount of meat.

The late afternoon sun was casting long shadows as the four slowly moved the single animal away from the herd. They were able to guide it toward the area where the rest of the team sat watching.

The animal Taelo and Golden Hawk were slowly herding back toward the camp. The buffalo finally reached a point where it wanted to return to the herd. They were about half the way back to the place where everyone was sitting around the fire watching the hunt.

"It looks like that will be about as far as they can move this animal," Little Otter commented to the watching team members

"I am betting they will get it even closer," Burley Bear replied.

"Let's guess how close they will bring the beast to where we are. The one that is closest to the drop point does not have to help in the cleaning and skinning," Talking Wren suggested.

"I pick by the fire pit," she continued.

Everyone quickly picked a drop spot. As if it had been planned, they saw Taelo and Golden Hawk jump off their mounts and run besides the animal to keep it coming toward them.

They guided the young bull past the surprised group watching them and then past Saber Scar and the group coming back to help skin the bull.

"What in the blue moon is coming toward us," Floating Cloud said as she jumped up and grabbed her spear.

"It's one of the new animals we saw earlier," Lily cried out as she too grabbed her spear.

"Now," Taelo called out at the last moment and both he and Golden Hawk ran out ahead of the animal, planted their spear in the ground and let the young bull spear itself.

The bull fell to its front knees and slid toward the fire pit and collapsed just a spear's length from it.

Both Lily and Floating Cloud started laughing. They were a little hysterical but none the less laughing.

As the team rode in, Talking Wren shouted out that she had won.

Little Otter questioned her claim. Talking Wren pointed out that the animal was near the fire ring as she had bet.

She got off and ran to Taelo and gave him a hug and whispered, "I did mean the fire out by the hunt site."

She again made the point that she had said by the fire, and she pointed to the young bull kneeling in front of the fire.

What was the wager," Quiet Rabbit asked?

"The one who guessed the closest drop location did not have to help in the skinning and cleaning," Burley Bear replied.

"Well, it would seem that unless someone chose a location closer to this camp, Talking Wren wins no matter what fire the bull came closest to," Busy Bee said.

The entire team broke out laughing.

"Yes, we declare Talking Wren the winner and we know we will hear about this for many moon cycles," Meadow Flower and Marigold said in unison as they each gave Talking Wren a hug.

The next sun cycle Feather-in-the-Wind, Running Stag, Slow Runner and Lily went as a team for the second buffalo.

"It was generous of Taelo to give us a turn," Slow Runner said as he and Running Stag prepared to cull out the next animal.

"I am so excited to accompany you," Lily said as she was handed the hunting spear she would carry for Slow Runner.

"And I am so happy to be recovered enough to go out with Running Stag," Feather-in-the-Wind almost sang her words as she was handing Running Stag his spear.

"This is a great way to get Feather-in-the-Wind back into action," Talking Wren commented as the team watched the four ride out toward the herd.

"Everyone on this team is deserving of recognition. We all contribute and share the work equally. We succeed because of our actions," Taelo replied.

On her return, Feather-in-the-Wind told the team how good it felt to be back up to speed. She thanked them for having taken such good care of her.

For the next three sun cycles each hunt team went out for a buffalo. The meat was processed and put on the sleds for transport.

The following morning began with the cry of the eagle. Everyone was up and looking at the sky at the eagle highlighted by the rising sun.

It gave out another cry and flew off into the distance.

"I think we should go that way, Little Otter and Burley Bear both said in unison as they together pointed in the direction the eagle had flown. They had come to know that the team always followed in the direction of the eagle flight.

Feather-in-the-Wind now refreshed and energized led the team in the direction the eagle had flown. Her sling was once again busy as she bagged a variety of small game. She had seen a mix of the woolly buffalo, the new elk, fox, rabbits, and birds.

The team reached a point where it was clear that before them lay the ice bridge that had been foretold by Broken Spear.

On closer inspection it was clear that the mounts could not be taken across.

The team would need to proceed on wolf drawn sleds.

Lily volunteered to stay and manage the mounts. She, Slow Runner, Single Leaf and Sharp Blade had agreed to stay.

Feather-in-the-Wind and Running Stag found a place where the teams lodge could be set up for them. It also had an area that could easily be fenced off to hold the mounts.

The team hunted enough buffalo that both the team staying behind and those going across the ice bridge would have enough meat.

The team members staying with the mounts was a change of plans. This brought up the question of what the team would face on the other side of the ice bridge.

Running Stag and Lily described the land on the other side. The confrontation with the Sky Eyes, foretold by Broken Spear surfaced as a point of concern.

Little Otter pointed out that on the team's trip to Feather-in-the-Wind's homeland, the team had defeated a superior force. The team had practiced being ready for that attack. He wondered what the team should do to get ready for the upcoming confrontation.

Feather-in-the-Wind suggested that their sleds be arranged in a circle and with their wolves loose, the team would be able to defend themselves against an attack. The team could also employ the fighting diamond and use the wolves to attack from the outside and from behind the attackers.

The discussion continued until the team closed in on a series of plans based on the situation, they found themselves in.

Feather-in-the-Wind and the rest of the team participated in designing the practice sessions for the agreed to scenarios.

The vast plain beyond the small river, now white in fresh knee-high winter snow that was interrupted only by the occasional enormous boulder and a few wind-blown knurly scruffy trees seemed to collide with the darker wall of the mountains and the greyer snow and ice blanketing them.

The backs of the ten wolves, their tails in the air, the centerline rope out to lead wolf harmonically separated the team as they effortlessly pulled the sled out from the campsite.

Feather-in-the-Wind looked back at the large canopy cover nestled into the vertical semi-circle of the solid stone face of the small cliff. A stonewall half the height to the canopy roof curved around from the cliff face to the door opening. The vertical leather of the canopy was attached along the outside bottom of the wall. The fresh snow had been pushed up along the outside of this wall and packed down to provide insulation against the cold.

A fire ring intended only for warming was just inside the leather lodge opening. The opening had a leather covered, stout wooden frame that locked into the slots at the end of the stonewalls.

A lighter frame, woven from willow branches taken from the willow trees found along the small stream running past the front of the compound area, went along the top of the stonewall and created an impenetrable wall that rose vertically a spear and a half in height to the edge of the canopy roofline. Poles ran radially out from the center pole to vertical poles located at the peripheral stonewall. These poles were in turn supported by additional vertical poles to ensure the roof would not collapse under the weight of heavy snow.

A huge pile of wood just past the fire ring ensured the four team members remaining behind would have enough wood for most of the coming cold period.

Lily, Slow Runner, Single Leaf and Sharp Blade stood by the fire ring that was a spear length from the compound opening. They remained behind and would take care of the mounts.

They waved their goodbye.

Out beyond the four, Feather-in-the-Wind took in the log and stone wall that enclosed the mount holding area. Her personal small mount stood looking in her direction. She had given it a morning treat before leaving.

She waved at the four, let out a loud Hi eee and held on to the sled as it shot forward.

The journey to and across the ice bridge was underway.

The team came to a halt when Burley Bear stopped his lead sled. He pointed to his left to a deep crevasse in the ice.

She listened as Taelo decided to take the lead and let Lasher pick his way. The only directional reference the team would have was the sun.

Lasher would periodically take a slightly different route and the team would follow.

Five sun cycles later Feather-in-the-Wind noted the descent toward a flat plain and then small brush and bend over wind-blown trees greeted the team.

The land was still snow covered, but the team moved into a full forest of bent, wind-blown trees.

She thanked Lasher with a small piece of meat for having brought the team across. Bold Walker, her lead sled wolf also got her thanks.

"I like the simplicity of this camp design. It lets us determine the size of our camp site and whether we want our wolf teams in with us or outside our camp perimeter," Feather-in-the-Wind commented with her arms around Bold Walker.

She was relieved and happy to set up the shelter for Running Stag and her. She gave him a hug and whispered; we are in your land now.

Chapter 16:

Feather-in-the-Wind listened as the next morning Golden Hawk asked why Running Stag's clan had crossed the Ice Bridge.

Running Stag replied that his clan was trying to escape the attacks of a large clan of cannibals. His clan fought a losing battle and really did not know where they were going. His clan was trying to get away.

"Do you think some of the cannibals still exist," Burley Bear asked?

"Yes, was Running Stag's reply. The ones Taelo and the team later defeated when we rescued the second group of my people were only a part of the cannibal clan," Running Stag continued.

"We may face them here and we are ready. However, I am more worried about meeting the Sky Eyed Clan," Saber Scar volunteered.

"The Sky Eyed Clan is the one that Broken Spear warned us about.

If we have a confrontation, we will fight a retreat and defend battle. The goal of each encounter will be to inflict deep wounds and then retreat. We will not allow them to use their superior force or fighting ability.

I want us to practice this way of fighting. One moment we will be invincible and the next we will be gone.

Our wolves will provide the distraction as we do this. Feather-in-the-Wind and Running Stag will be their commanders. They will need to be able to run as fast as the wolves.

Are you two up to this task," Taelo asked as he walked slowly around the campfire?

"Yes, I am ready. Will Lasher be part of our army," Feather-in-the-Wind inquired?

"Yes, he will join Walker and Arrow to protect the two of you," Taelo said as he petted Lasher.

The terrain slowly changed to a wooded landscape of mixed tall straight pines and a new dominant tree that provided an opening to the sun above. The few yellow fan-like leaves clinging pluckily to their branch identified it as a totally new kind of tree. Feather-in-the-Wind named it Ginkgo after the shape of braids worn by the young girls in the mountains of the Condor.

The snow still deep and thick was firm and the sleds sped smoothly along the top surface. The hunting had improved as they had entered this more prosperous area and the team was once again benefitting from Feather-in-the-Winds skill with her sling. Rabbits, squirrels, dove and many pigeons graced the end of a spit and got roasted over the cooking fire.

When the eagle high in the sky, screamed, Taelo knew that the calm before the storm was over.

"I think our first confrontation with the Blue Eyes is close at hand," he said to Golden Hawk and the rest of the team.

He turned to Running Stag and Feather-in-the-Wind and asked them to take the wolves out to the right side of the path they would take and told them to keep out of sight.

The eagle let out its scream as it circled in the clear sky.

"We must be close," Burley Bear called out from his lead position.

Taelo and Golden Hawk moved forward on each side of Burly Bear.

Running Stag and Feather-in-the-Wind and all the wolves were out of sight.

"I will walk out ahead. It appears they are coming out to fight not to talk. If you see me take any aggressive action move forward and strike.

From her hidden location in the tall grass on the top of the hill, Feather in the Wind watched as Taelo walked out ahead of the team.

He walked slowly toward a very tall well-proportioned man walking toward him.

"I am Taelo," Taelo said as he raised his open right hand above his head.

Feather-in-the-Wind thought back to the time Taelo had stood in front of the huge bear. This was another moment when he looked small in comparison to the animal standing in front of him.

He was looking up, at a very muscular person with rippled stomach muscles who was a head taller than Burley Bear.

The sky eyes were a light color but there was no kindness showing.

She watched as Taelo purposely stopped a weapon's distance away and his hand was open to show friendship but positioned to pull out his shark toothed flat weapon.

"I am Angry Cougar," the sky eyed person shouted as he lunged forward with the spear, he intended to plunge through the lithe but weak looking person.

She heard Taelo let out his loud war cry, as he took a measured step back and to the side and pulled his shark tooth weapon from its holder and cutoff the hand holding the spear.

She watched as the look of realization came to the sky eyed person standing in front of Taelo.

The action was lightening swift, and the result was a surprise to the attacker and to Taelo was well.

She and the entire team let out the same war cry. She and the wolves stayed out of sight. The rest of the team moved forward as the sky eyed leader that she would later learn was named, Angry Cougar, stumbled back holding his left hand over the stump where his missing right hand had once been. He was trying to stop the bleeding from the stump.

Angry Cougar's men rushed forward as his friend Rolling Stone ran out and tended to him.

The front line of brown eyed warriors that had been in front of the blue-eyed fighters hung back.

Taelo's team in its impenetrable wedge greeted the forty or so rushing warriors.

Burley Bear's hammer took down the first warrior to reach him. The story was much the same around the triangular wedge that slowly formed into an oval as the team retreated.

Once back to the top of the hill, Taelo looked around in concern and asked if anyone was injured?

You were the only one in danger by staying out in front," Quiet Rabbit replied.

"I couldn't make it back to the triangle with all the warriors coming at me. It is clear they have not thought through their battle plans. They will be better organized the next time they attack," Taelo replied.

"I did not plan to take the action that I took.

The person in front of me made the mistake of looking at where he planned to strike me.

He never saw my weapon until it cutoff his hand.

It is clear that he was their leader by the response of the rest of his warriors," Taelo continued explaining.

"We did not expose our wolf army, so we still have an element of surprise," Golden Hawk commented as the team continued their retreat back up the hill behind them.

"We will have to take a round-about way of returning to the sleds. These Sky Eyes may still come after us today," Burley Bear added

"Taelo has gone out to discuss our situation with Feather-in-the-Wind and Running Stag. We will want to disrupt the next attack. It will be more organized now that they know we can fight." Golden Hawk continued.

Feather-in-the-Wind listened as Taelo asked Running Stag to go to the village area and learn what he could about the situation.

She heard him inform the rest of the team. She had returned with him but the wolves were all still hidden in the tall grass.

"Lasher, Walker and I will manage the wolves," Feather-in-the-Wind had volunteered.

"Do you think Lasher will let me be with him," Talking Wren asked?

"Yes, thank you that will let me signal silently for your attack. That way we can surprise them twice," Feather-in-the-Wind replied.

Across the valley, Running Stag and Arrow crept silently through the forest that surrounded the village. It was located near a small river at the end of a slender valley.

He stopped short when he spotted another person watching the village. It soon became clear to him, as he watched the village, that the warriors that looked like those on Taelo's team were in fact more captives than voluntary participants.

He remembered his village being taken by the cannibals.

It appeared the Blue Eyes had taken over the village.

"The person I am watching, as he watches the village, is probably an escaped member. I am sure he is trying to figure out what to do," Running Stag thought to himself.

When he saw the war party leave the village, he quickly retreated and made his way as fast as he could back to the team.

He reported to the team that the brown eyed warriors were being used as a front shield as Taelo had previously conjectured and that the entire village was under the control of the Blue Eyes. There was another watcher, that was also watching the village.

"Can you find these other people," Taelo inquired?

"We can use their help."

"Yes, I can find them, but I am not sure how may there may be," Running Stag replied.

"We will be able to use any help we can get," Taelo replied.

"I will leave immediately and retrace my steps. I hope I am able to communicate enough with them to get them here," Running Stag said as he gathered his gear.

This time he left Arrow with Feather-in-the-Wind.

He set out on a run back to where he had been and followed the tracks he found in the snow.

The hill offered Feather-in-the-Wind a clear view of the small valley all the way to the village located along the small winding river. The bare branches of the broadleaf trees allowed a spotty view of the camp but the density of the ever green blocked the view to the point that it was impossible to see what was transpiring.

She could not be sure but periodically she thought she saw Running Stag as he ran full speed through the thick forest. She hoped he would not be too reckless in his haste to reach the group of people that might help in the coming battle.

Meadow Flower with her superior eyesight could see the turmoil and what seemed to be preparation for a return to the field by the Sky Eyed warriors.

Her self-confidence was raised as she turned to listen to Taelo and saw him sitting in a relaxed manner on a small boulder.

Taelo was explaining to the team that they would fight from the top slope of the hill. The goal was to make the larger and stronger Sky Eyes come up to them.

Talking Wren would have half of the wolves to one side and Feather-in-the-Wind would have the other half on the other side.

If Running Stag was successful there would be an attack from the rear. That will provide for total chaos.

She listened as Taelo told the team he knew they would face a superior force. The team's main weapon would be a surprise and a disruption to how the Sky Eyes normally fought their battles.

He made the point that he would delay as long as possible to allow Running Stag to recruit the help of the escaped villagers.

Running Stag back tracked as fast as he could run. Once back to where he had seen the other watcher, he followed the tracks away from the village up-river to an area full of tumbled stones.

As he came through a narrow opening, he was faced with a small group all defensively holding their spears.

"I am here as a friend," he said in his childhood language, as he faced the group.

"How do you know our language," someone asked?

"I was born not far from here, but our clan had to flee from a group of savage cannibals," Running Stag replied.

"Yes, we had to fight them as well," one of the older warriors commented.

"I am Whistling Arrow, a hunter and warrior in my youth and now advisor to the council," Whistling Arrow introduced himself.

"I have returned here with Taelo on a Journey of Discovery. We need your help to fight the Sky Eyes. They have already lost but don't yet know it. If you join us, I will lead you back and we will attack them from the rear," Running Stag continued.

There were only nine men and twelve women. There were at least a dozen younger children. Several of the men were well beyond the age for running and going into battle. There were also several older women.

"We are willing to help. What do you want us to do?"

"Some of you will need to stay with the young and some of you have already done your duty in battle.

Those who can run from here to the valley beyond your village, line up and show me the best weapon you have.

All of you will be needed," Running Stag said as he took in the situation.

"You would take women into battle," Gentle Cub, one of the young women inquired?

"Yes, some of our best fighters are women," Running Stag replied.

There were sixteen viable candidates.

Running Stag led them out and ran at a slow but steady pace. He kept dropping back and urging them on.

"When we arrive, we will attack from the back of the battle. When we attack, I want each of you to yell at the top of your voices. Cut your attackers on the back of their legs or spear them in their sides. Do not try to kill anyone, just wound them.

Those of you with stone war clubs hit your opponent on the back of his skull and then drop down and hit the next enemy on his knee.

Then jump up again," Running Stag instructed the group. He was doing all he could to get them ready and to be able to survive.

"When we get there and run forward into the battle, tell your friends to turn and fight against the Sky Eyes," Running Stag told them.

"I hope we arrive in time to make a difference," Running Stag thought as he worried about Feather-in-the-Wind.

He knew she was fearless and would take on any of the Blue Eyes.

His fear for Feather-in the-Wind was misplaced.

Taelo meanwhile was positioning the team and getting them in the position on the hill where they would remain throughout the battle. Then he told the team to sit and relax. He asked Talking Wren and Feather-in-the-Wind to get out of sight in the tall grass on each side of the hill.

"Stay until I say "Kill" Taelo faintly heard Feather-in-the-Wind give instruction to Lasher and Walker. Lasher lay down flat and his entire pack did likewise. Talking Wren lay beside Lasher.

"Thanks for humoring me," Talking Wren whispered to Lasher as she scratched him between the ears.

Feather-in-the-Wind disappeared down into the tall grass and Bold Walker and his part of the pack did the same.

"Truly a gifted wolf woman," Taelo said quietly as he looked out to where the Sky Eyes were coming up the valley.

"I wonder what they are saying about us," Busy Bee commented next.

She was surprised at how relaxed she was.

"They no doubt think we are crazy," Meadow Flower added.

"The longer we can delay them the more likely we will get some help coming with Running Stag," Golden Hawk commented from his position.

"Please be so kind as to wake me up when something is about to happen," Burly Bear said with a faked yawn.

"I hope they get mad enough to misjudge their actions. They seem to be getting frustrated by being ignored," Quiet Rabbit commented as she studied the arrangement of the oncoming warriors.

"It appears they expect us to charge them, and they don't seem to know what to do because we are just sitting here," Marigold commented.

"Stop, get down and be quiet. The fighting has not started," Running Stag said as his group came to the edge of the forest. He was glad they had a moment to rest.

"Why are your people just sitting at top of the hill," one of the warriors asked?

"I am sure it is Taelo's way of disrupting the Sky Eyes battle plans. The Sky Eyes do not know how to act. When you are outnumbered ten to one you must use every trick in the book," Running Stag replied.

"Ten to one, do we even have a chance," one of the women asked?

"The Sky Eyes have already lost the battle. They just do not yet know it.

Half of them will go to their ancestors when they go up that hill.

The rest will be lucky if they get away," Running Stag commented as he let out a wolf howl.

High in the sky an eagle responded with a loud screaming reply.

"Our teammate Running Stag is in position and our eagle has given us its signal. We will soon face out next test," Taelo said quietly.

He was worried about this weird situation and about the meaning of the eagle's cry.

Taelo surprised everyone by standing up and walking a few steps forward toward the Sky Eyes coming up the hill.

He raised his hand and, in the language Running Stag had taught him, he called out loudly, "My brown eyed brothers, the eagle is my totem. He has spoken to all of us, but he has given me the sign of victory. Come as close as you can to us. Put bravery in your hearts and help us fight the Sky Eyes that have enslaved you. The people of your village are behind you, and they will help. This is your moment. This is the moment to be brave. When you hear my battle cry, you will know that it is your moment as well. Victory will be yours"

Taelo then turned, stepped back, turned, and sat down with his back to the oncoming hoard of warriors.

"I think the battle plan just changed. We will put the stone shards in the Blue Eyes first. Meadow Flower and Marigold please give us a hand," Quiet Rabbit said quietly from where she sat.

"With pleasure," the two responded in unison.

"Yes, if the brown eye warriors fight with us, they will be spared the pain of your shards," Golden Hawk commented.

"Burley Bear let me know when it is time to stand and give my war cry," Taelo said with a smile on his face.

A short time later Burley Bear quietly said, "Now."

Taelo stood, slowly turned around and let out the team's battle cry. The team repeated three pulsing cries in unison at the top of their voice. The volume of their war cry surprised the on-coming hoard of Sky Eye warriors. They almost stopped in their tracks.

"Run forward brothers and turn and fight," Taelo said in Running Stag's language as he stepped out to the front and raised his spear.

"Now," Quiet Rabbit said as she let her first sling loose and hit Angry Cougar in the Face.

His scream and reflex action of his right arm with the missing hand almost knocked him out.

The disorienting impact of the barrage of sharp stone fragments in the face almost stopped the charge.

However, the warriors in the back ran past those trying to recover. They were just getting ready to launch their first set of spears when Talking Wren stood up and Lasher led his wolves in from the left side of the Sky Eyes battle line.

The warriors had to turn and defend themselves from the oncoming pack of wolves.

One set of warriors reached the team's fighting triangle. They were focused on fighting with their war hammers and were surprised by the combination of the shark tooth weapons and the war hammer of the Others.

Burley Bear, Meadow Flower, Saber Scar and Marigold made a devastating combination. The bodies of dead Sky Eyed warriors piled up around them.

Taelo had three bodies around him. He noted that the brown eyes had turned and were fighting with them.

The battle was still on the side of the Sky Eye warriors when Feather-in-the-Wind rose from the grass and her wolf warriors charged the right side of the Sky Eye warriors.

Once again, the Blue Eye's attack was dulled and the warriors around the fighting triangle met the ultimate fate. They were no match for the synchronized action of Taelo's team.

Angry Cougar's eyes were just clearing when he saw Taelo raise his sharks tooth weapon and let out his war cry again.

The team around Taelo echoed his cry and then to Angry Cougar's surprise the cry came from behind him.

Running Stag and his team had run silently across the valley. When Taelo had let out his second battle cry, Running Stag responded, and all those following him took it up and continued the cry as they ran through the ranks of Sky Eye warriors.

Running Stag concentrated on using his sharks tooth weapon across the back of the heel of the warriors. This did not kill any of them, but it took them out of the battle. He took out more than his share as he went through the line of warriors.

Angry Cougar saw his warriors falling all around him.

"Run for the forest. Retreat so we can regroup," he called out.

"Bring the wounded with you," Rolling Stone called out.

High in the sky the eagle again let out its cry and flew effortlessly away.

Bodies lay strewn down the hillside. The snow was now a bright red. There were no bodies with black hair or brown skin. There were only Blue Eyes now sightlessly looking up into the bright sun at its zenith.

The team watched as the few able Sky Eyes helped their wounded away from the field of battle. They were headed into the mountains to the west.

Taelo counted ten warriors carrying ten badly wounded ones.

He watched Burley Bear, Meadow Flower and Quiet Rabbit going through the battlefield checking on the fallen.

It seemed they would be done for the day.

The fighting was over.

"Running Stag, you and Golden Hawk organize our friends and determine what we must do to get them their village back.

Quiet Rabbit, Busy Bee, Marigold and Meadow Flower, please check each of our warriors and attend to their wounds.

Talking Wren, Feather-in-the-Wind please check out our wolves. Let Busy Bee know of your needs.

Burley Bear, Little Otter and Saber Scar please check each of the Sky Eyes that remain in the field. If they are not dead, do not kill them. Call Quiet Rabbit to check their condition. We will see what can be done," Taelo said as he visually checked out each of his team members.

He then arranged for all the dead to be buried on the hill on which they had died.

"Who is that man," one of the brown eyed warriors asked?

"That is our leader, Taelo, claw of the eagle," Feather-in-the-Wind replied.

Chapter 17:

Deer Chaser, one the young men in the village, asked Running Stag if the remaining White Bear Clan members could join Taelo and his team. He explained how on the very first day the White Bear Clan leader was killed as he greeted the Sky Eye leader. Our other leaders refused to follow the Sky Eyes and were killed on that same day.

Running Stag replied that he would let Taelo know of the request.

Gentle Cub one of the young women who had engaged in the battle asked if she and Deer Chaser could go to Taelo to plead their case.

"Why don't the two of you organized your clan and discuss this issue. In the next few sun cycles, you can bring your request to Taelo, and a decision can be reached. That way he will know that everyone in your clan had a chance to make a choice," Running Stag suggested.

"These visitors seem so progressive. Their women fight with them in battle. They are very organized, and they trust young men like

Running Stag to talk to us and guide us," Whistling Arrow, one of the few remaining elders, said to Gentle Cub and the people standing around him.

"I would like to be guided by the leaders who are willing to engage all their people so openly," Whistling Arrow continued.

Feather-in-the-Wind listened to Running Stag's description of his interaction with the people in the village. She approached Quiet Rabbit and Busy Bee and discussed the desire of the White Bear Clan members wanting to return with them. She was confident that if the two were sympathetic and supportive then the request would be positively received by Taelo and Golden Hawk.

Taelo immediately agreed to take the White Bear Clan back across the ice bridge. He pointed out that the bear and dire wolf population in the Elk Clan's territory was larger than the population of the Elk Clan.

He asked her, Running Stag, Golden Hawk, Busy Bee, Little Otter and Talking Wren to guide the White Bear Clan to the ice bridge. He planned to take the rest of the team into the mountains to the northwest as a decoy to attract an attack by the remaining Sky Eyes. He knew the battle would only end when the Sky Eye leader was dead.

He left half of the sleds to help in the transport of the village possessions, but he made the point that the villagers would need to use travois to transport the less important items.

He asked Golden Hawk to lead the White Bear Clan to hunt for buffalo during the next moon cycle to prepare for the trip back across the ice bridge.

Feather-in-the-Wind took note of how thorough Taelo was in making sure that all the necessary and critical items were addressed. He did not get into the details of how everything was to get done. It was clear that he counted on each individual to determine how each task would get done.

It took six sun cycles for the team to make the arrangements and to redistribute the food to each person of the White Bear Clan.

"Will we cross over the ice bridge during the cold months," Saber Scar asked?

Taelo replied that the goal would be to spend the remainder of winter with Lily, Slow Runner, Sharp Blade and Single Leaf.

Feather-in-the-Wind thought about her mount and looked forward to riding it when she and Running Stag went to hunt the northern buffalo. She was ready to return to the land she now called home.

On the sun cycle of their departure to the ice bridge, Busy Bee commented on the beauty of the day.

The cry of an eagle seemed to Feather-in-the-Wind to be a reply. She wondered if it was signaling Taelo and if the expected confrontation with the Sky Eyes was taking place. She had watched as Golden Hawk left with Running Stag's bow and arrows. He said he had been called by ancients to help Taelo and he would need to do so from afar.

Busy Bee had wished him well and told him to let his aim be true. "They are each-others, keepers. I am his mate, but Taelo and he are of the same soul," Busy Bee said quietly to her as she watched Golden Hawk jog across the valley.

Feather-in-the-Wind knew that Taelo would not know that Golden Hawk was shadowing him.

The first rays of sun came rapidly over the mountains and morning burst into full bloom. It was a beautiful day and a day full of worry for Busy Bee.

Feather-in-the-Wind took the lead. She and Running Stag communicated directly with the White Bear Clan members. They worked hard at keeping everyone moving. It was their goal to lighten the load for Busy Bee.

Somewhere an eagle let out a scream. Busy Bee searched the sky but could not see it.

"Perhaps the eagle does cry out for you Golden Hawk as well as for Taelo," she thought to herself.

The eagle cry was heard by the caravan of the White Bear Clan.

"I travel with a lighter heart," Busy Bee commented to Feather-in-the-Wind and Talking Wren.

Feather-in-the-Wind saw a look of relief in Busy Bee's face.

The earlier than usual fall snows had conditioned the team to winter hunting and making camp in the frigid cold. The rising wind, the dark grey clouds in the sky and the dimming of the light at midday warned of a powerful impending winter storm.

The tall pines bent and swung around as the wind began its assault along the sharp ravine through the mountains.

The snow on the ground began to follow the flow of the wind and piled up against tree trunks, boulders and any obstacle that would hold the snow back.

A major blizzard fully loaded with snow from the moist warm air from the west meeting the cold air from the east was forming overhead.

"We must beat the cold winter weather and get across the ice bridge and set up our winter lodge," Feather-in-the-Wind commented to Running Stag.

It was as if her words awoke the winter storm. From the east an almost black sky moved in with a vengeance. The sky turned a mean dead dark grey color, and the wind began to howl.

"I will go out ahead and find a place for us to stop," Running Stag volunteered and moved his sled into the lead.

Feather-in-the-Wind moved among the White Bear Clan members and explained what needed to get done once they arrived at the place that she was sure Running Stag would find.

Running Stag crossed a small river and proceeded to inspect a large grouping of rocks and boulders near the river. He noted the stand of small trees and willows. These would be very useful in setting up a secure camp.

"Let's hope we have enough time to get our shelter built," Running Stag thought to himself as he turned his wolf team around and raced back.

"This looks like a good spot," Talking Wren agreed after crossing the small river and inspecting the area.

"Put the sleds in a semi-circle around those large boulders. Get some poles between the boulders to hold the covering hides and tie the other edges to the outside of the sleds. Leave an opening for a door in the middle," Talking Wren directed.

"You six; gather all the grasses you can and fill the opening between the sleds," Feather-in-the-Wind instructed as she began to cut the tall grass along the bank of the river.

"Let's fill in between the boulders with a combination of rocks and grasses. We will want to keep the wind and snow out," she continued as she led her team in getting the grasses cut and put into place.

"Let's get a fire ring made and all the wood you can find gathered and piled next to it," Running Stag directed as he led another group.

"A few of you follow me to the river. We will gather as many long poles as possible," Little Otter instructed as he walked down to the river's edge.

Feather-in-the-Wind repeatedly consulted with Busy Bee, Talking Wren and Little Otter. She and Running Stag concentrated in guiding the work of the White Bear Clan members.

Soon the entire clan was working swiftly to get the shelter ready.

"Leave this open between these two sleds. This will be where the wolves will come and go," Busy Bee commented as Feather-in-the-Wind's team finished sealing the wall made by the sleds and the stonewall.

The cover was attached to the outer edges of the sleds and held up poles that been strategically positioned.

"Let's get everyone and the wolves inside. Then we can send the cooks and guards out to prepare a meal," Busy Bee instructed.

"Thanks for bring up the support timbers. Let's get them positioned to support the hide roof," Running Stag said as he indicated where to put each support pole.

"Let's hope Taelo and the rest of the team found some good shelter. They did not have as many hides or shelter material with them as we have," Running Stag commented to Feather-in-the-Wind as he lay back and relaxed against one of the boulders.

The hide covering for the roof had a steep slope and many reinforcing timbers running from the top of the boulders to the outside edges of the sleds.

Running Stag remembered the lodge and had put vertical supporting poles in the key spots. He was confident these poles would keep the snow from collapsing the roof.

"I am confident that Taelo and the team will find a good spot to take shelter. In fact, we will need to ask them if Taelo and Golden Hawk found another hot spring as a shelter," Busy Bee joked. She knew that Golden Hawk and Taelo seemed to have a magic touch when it came to finding shelter.

She was concerned but she instinctively knew the two would keep the other part of the team safe.

There were almost one hundred people crowded into the small area. It was tight but everyone had enough room to lie down comfortably. With so many people in such a small area, keeping the inside of the shelter cool turned out to be the challenge.

"We will not need a fire for heating. We will need it to provide a little light," Busy Bee noted as she opened a leather flap between two boulders to let out the hot air.

"We will keep a path open down to the river, so everyone has a place to relieve themselves. Down river please! Up-river will be for our water supply," Feather-in-the-Wind instructed.

"Two persons will always remain awake and working. We will take turns going out and clearing the path to the river and pulling the snow off the shelter. I have talked to the eight persons who are assigned tonight and have instructed them in their duties," Little Otter announced.

"We have made the right choice in asking to go with this team," Deer Chaser commented.

"Yes, I agree. They seem to know exactly what to do with almost no communication between them. And notice they are unconcerned with who leads," Gentle Cub replied.

"I have seen many summers. I have never seen a group of people work so well together and know how to engage and lead those around them. Their leader seems to have created a metanoic team," Whistling Arrow commented.

"I agree and I feel confident that with them we are safe," Bubbling Brook added.

Feather-in-the-Wind nudged Running Stag as she heard the compliments being paid to them and the rest of Taelo's team. He simply grunted and asked what was new.

Along the river, the White Bear Clan was sitting quietly inside the enclosure.

"We will be eating a lot of our dried food," Busy Bee commented as she came in from the river. "We have another storm headed our way. Let's get everyone to go out and gather all the wood and any dried grass they can find."

"We are going to be short on food when we get a chance to move on toward the ice bridge," Running Stag commented quietly.

"Yes, I hope Quiet Rabbit, Taelo and Golden Hawk join up with us before then. They will have extra dried food though I don't think even that will be enough," Feather-in-the-Wind added.

"Let's get a few folks to go along the riverbank and gather enough small willow trees to make one of Taelo's fish traps," Busy Bee suggested.

"That is a great idea. We can spend the time during the storm to get the sticks ready and put up our fish trap immediately after the storm," Running Stag said as he got up and recruited a half a dozen young men.

"I think this is a little crazy. Here comes a mean storm and we are gathering young willow saplings," Deer Chaser commented to his assigned partner, as he slipped and fell into the river and came out with his teeth chattering.

"I am not sure about being crazy. Running Stag said this might well save our lives," replied White Bear.

"Well, I hope it's worth it to be out here as the storm hits. Let's get our bundle back to the camp before my clothes freeze in place and I can't walk," the wet and freezing Deer Chaser replied.

"Welcome back and good job," Talking Wren said handing each of the willow hunters a bowl of hot soup as they returned.

"Well, I go from being a complainer to feeling like a hero," Deer Chaser commented as he sat down with his bowl of soup. He took the time to peel off his wet clothes and put on some dry ones before taking a gulp of his soup.

"Thank you all for this great effort. We need to build up our food reserves. We think of ourselves as hunters, but Taelo always says that we are really fishermen.

We will prepare the saplings to build a fish trap. As soon as the storm passes, we will set up the trap. In the morning we will work together. Tonight, we will relax and let the storm howl as we sleep in our warm enclosure," Running Stag announced.

"Your mate demonstrates great leadership," Talking Wren commented to Feather-in-the-Wind.

"Yes, he is perfect, and he does exactly what I ask," Feather-in-the-Wind joked.

The morning sky was a fresh, clear cloudless blue. The lack of clouds made the day colder than it otherwise would have been.

"Each of us will take a turn wading out into the river and planting the stakes we have prepared. Once you get your stakes in place come immediately back to the fire, dry off and put on your warm clothes," Running Stag commented as he removed his coat and pants.

He waded into the water only wearing his loin cloth. He immediately began to turn blue in the bitter cold. Once he got his six poles in place he came charging back out and rushed to the fire.

The rest of the fish trap team followed his lead. A short time later they all watched as the first fish began to get trapped in the shallow pit they had made on their side of the river.

A cheer from the fish trap team caused everyone to take a look.

"I would not have believed this was possible," Gentle Cub commented as she and a team of the young women began to clean the fish being brought up to them.

"I have seen many things, but this is amazing," Whistling Arrow commented.

"This will certainly help to tide us over and may be the margin of safety we need. Let's dry half of what we catch and enjoy the other half as part of our normal meals," Busy Bee commented.

"I will organize the smoking and drying of the fish," Talking Wren volunteered.

Feather-in-the-Wind smiled at the talk that the White Bear Clan members shared with each other. She took note of the new hope and energy they were displaying.

"We should stay here as long as the fish keep coming in at this rate," Feather-in-the-Wind commented.

"I will volunteer to be the taste tester of any cooked or smoked fish," Little Otter said in a serious tone.

It was the end of the second day of fishing and the trap continued to deliver fish.

"I would not have believed we could have caught so many fish. The little ones are able to go through the trap. Only the larger fish end up in the pickup area," Deer Chaser noted.

"We will continue to the ice bridge on the second sun cycle from this one," Busy Bee announced.

It had been a hard decision to make but after discussion with the rest of the team they had agreed that they needed to take advantage of the good weather and travel on toward the ice bridge.

"I have the camp clean up assignments and will come around today and share them with each of you," Feather-in-the-Wind added.

"Do you see what I see," Running Stag said as he pointed out what appeared to be a buffalo trotting toward them.

"Yes, and I also see Golden Hawk and Taelo," White Cloud said as she took up her spear.

"It's time to bring this animal down," Golden Hawk said as two ran along behind the buffalo.

Taelo and Golden Hawk closed the gap to the buffalo. As anticipated, it took off at a full gallop and headed into the camp.

Both Taelo and Golden Hawk ran up ahead and simultaneously planted their spears. The young bull hit the spears and went sliding down on its knees within a spears throw of the camp's main cooking fire.

"I have never seen such skill. It is no surprise these two defeated the Sky Eyes," Deer Chaser commented to those around him.

"Yes, I have never seen anything like this," Whistling Arrow added.

Talking Wren had heard the comment and was glad that Taelo and Golden Hawk had displayed some of their many talents. This would be of great help later when the going became harder.

"It is great to see the two of you," Busy Bee commented as she gave them each a hug.

"Where is the rest of the team," Feather-in-the-Wind asked?

The coming together of friends is always a cause for celebration. The heart warms at seeing a friend. The joking and laughter are universal signs of the positive impact that friends have on one another.

Taelo's arrival not only brought the relief of enough food for the White Bear Clan, but he and Golden Hawk's presence gave immediate relief to the concern the group had for the missing members.

Just after the sun reached the horizon and the brightness of the day gave way to the dark, the rest of the team was seen racing in towards the camp.

Burley Bear's arrival with the rest of the team was a cause for celebration. The entire team was back together.

They were ready to tackle the passage across the ice bridge.

"I noted that you have set up a fish trap in the river. Has it been effective," Taelo inquired?

"Yes, we have gathered enough fish to feed the entire White Bear Clan for at least ten sun cycles and we have only eaten fish the past two sun cycles," Feather-in-the-Wind replied.

"It will take about two moon cycles to reach the ice bridge. We have more than ninety people to feed and as many wolves. The fish will help but we will need to send out two sleds to get four more buffalo," Taelo said as he shared the challenge of supplying the needs of this many people.

"I will be pleased to hunt with you," Saber Scar volunteered.

Taelo thanked him for volunteering, but he wanted to have Deer Chaser and White Bear to go out with he and Golden Hawk. He wanted to see if they could run fast enough to learn to hunt in the same manner as he and Golden Hawk.

He also shared the fact that he had also turned down, Quiet Rabbit, Busy Bee, Talking Wren, Feather-in-the-Wind and Running Stag.

Burley Bear and Little Otter both laughed and said that they preferred to stay and enjoy the comfort of the camp.

"I think that some language lessons are in order," Running Stag commented. "I remember Busy Bee teaching me. I would love to get these lessons started."

"I will teach the use of the sling. There are many rabbits and other small game we can be bagging as we travel," Feather-in-the-Wind said.

"I would love to learn to use the sling. It was amazing how you stopped the charge of the Sky Eyes with them," Gentle Cub commented when she understood what Feather-in-the-Wind had suggested.

"And I will lead the cooking class. Every member of this clan will cook a meal for all of us as we travel," Quiet Rabbit spoke up.

"Let's prepare this clan to become productive Elk Clan members. Our return should coincide with the Elk Clan end of hunting season gathering. Once again, we will arrive with the equivalent of another clan. We must prepare the White Bear Clan members to be mixed with the other sub-clans," Golden Hawk added.

"We can prepare the young women and single men as we did two cycles ago. Almost all the young women found mates during the gathering," Feather-in-the-Wind volunteered as she thought of all the proposals she had received and had turned down.

"I think your ideas are wonderful," Whistling Arrow replied when Running Stag shared what was being discussed.

Whistling Arrow had wondered what all the discussion was about.

"I especially like the idea of the language lessons. We need to be able to talk to ensure we all understand what is happening," Bending Willow added

"Let's sit down and lay out our plans," Burley Bear said as he gathered them back around their warming fire.

"Running Stag, you translate for Whistling Arrow and Bending Willow. I want them to help us get organized," Burley Bear continued.

"I would like six people assigned to our fish trap. Pick those that can take the cold water and recover quickly. They will fish at every stream we cross on our way to the ice bridge. We will assign one sled to them. They will fish as we travel and will catch up or go ahead of us as is needed," Burley Bear put his request to Whistling Arrow.

"We will want all of the clan to learn to use the sling and gather small game as we travel. I will be the primary teacher, but our entire team is very good and any of us can and will teach as we travel," Feather-in-the-Wind added in Running Stag's language.

She was as fluent as Taelo and had spent many hours talking to the White Bear Clan members.

Running Stag translated to the Elk Clan language and then went on to do it in the language of the Others.

"Ok, I guess we know who will be assisting me in teaching the Elk Clan language to everyone," Busy Bee commented as she pointed to Running Stag and Feather-in-the-Wind.

"Oh, I am going to be too busy with my sling lessons," Feather-in-the-Wind bantered back.

She had already been engaged in teaching her language to a few of the young women.

Feather-in-the-Wind had spent the time in the tight quarters learning about the White Bear Clan. There were fifty young members, twenty older members, fifteen children and only an additional six paired couples.

She had already been engaged in teaching her language to a few of the young women.

Chapter 18:

Looking up from below, the sunlight created a long glowing narrow ceiling that bridged the bottomless miles long fissure in the ice. This fissure was invisible from above. It blended in with the rest of the endless white expanse bridging the land in the west to the land to the east. Many such thin ice bridges or ceilings dotted the path across to the land on the other side. To fall through, was to fall to one's doom. Throwing an object in and counting until it hit bottom was useless. The fissures were so deep that the sound was never heard.

They were as deep as death.

The sun traveled its course for another forty cycles before the group arrived at the ice bridge. It was really a wide expanse of ice with many dangerous cracks and bubbles where the periodic warming rays of the sun had melted the ice and it had sunk down. There were also large cracks made by the uneven movement of individual ice plates.

Feather-in-the-Wind and Running Stag had selected the children and some of the young women to ride in the now empty food sleds.

Taelo had expressed his desire to have more food for the crossing but knew he had to cross as soon as possible.

The team made camp at what they took as the beginning of the ice bridge.

"With all this snow, I am worried about our ability to find a safe passage across," Golden Hawk spoke up during their dinner.

"I will take the lead," Taelo replied.

"We need to worry about falling into some hidden crevasse. If your wolves start to fall through the snow, lay your sled down on its side and drive your spear down into the snow in front of the sled handles," Burley Bear instructed as he entered into the conversation.

Feather-in-the-Wind watched as Taelo went to his sled and flipped the solidly loaded sled on its side and drove his spear into the ground just ahead of the sleds handles.

"Is this what you are telling me," Taelo asked looking at Burley Bear?

"As always, you practice the actions that are needed," Burley Bear replied.

He thanked Burley Bear for the information.

Just then the cry of the eagle was heard.

As the entire group looked up into the sky, Quiet Rabbit expressed her concern.

"What does this mean," Whistling Arrow asked?

"We are never sure of the exact meaning. The cry came before we fought with the Sky Eyes. It comes before every challenge the team faces," Busy Bee replied.

"Let's have each of the sled driver's practice laying their sleds on their sides and anchoring them with their spear," Saber Scar instructed.

He was now more eager to practice this life saving maneuver.

"Yes, let's do it three times," Little Otter and Burley Bear said in unison.

The next morning the journey across the ice bridge began. On the team's first crossing it had taken six cycles of the sun.

"We will need to be much more cautious on our way back across. The new snow covering will hide many of the crevasses that were very easy to see before," Taelo commented.

"Let's tie our sleds together. If one of them begins to go through the ice we can keep it from going down," Little Otter suggested.

He recalled the trip through the blinding snow where they had tied the sleds together during their rescue of the people from the north.

"Great idea, it saved us the last time," Running Stag said in support.

"Yes, and I brought in the rest of people by tying them together so I would not lose any. We will go across in single line formation. Whistling Arrow let's tie a rope from each person to the one behind them. You will follow behind the last sled," Taelo added

"Ok, I think we are now ready. The first four sleds will have our food and other materials. The other four have our young," Taelo said as he and Quiet Rabbit took the lead.

"Be careful where you walk," Taelo called up to Lasher.

When the team stopped for their evening meal, Talking Wren commented on the good progress they had made.

There was no wood for cooking. They were out on a pure layer of ice. Their meal consisted of dry fish and meat.

As the sun rose above the horizon and the team got ready to get under way, Golden Hawk commented that the way ahead looked more challenging than the previous day.

The entire caravan moved slowly across the ice. They followed Taelo as he maneuvered around several ice spikes and areas where the ice had pushed up like small mountains. The way remained challenging for the entire morning. Then as the sun reached its zenith they came out into a flat area for as far as the eye could see.

"I hope this is…"Taelo began to speak and then Lasher disappeared.

Horror was the only description of the feeling that swept over Feather-in-the-Wind as her mind registered what was happening.

She watched Taelo fling Quite Rabbit, through the air, almost three spear lengths back to where Quiet Rabbit hit Burley Bear's lead wolf.

Even as his sled was being pulled into crevasse, Taelo looped his tie rope and drove his spear into the snow and ice. Then he stepped on to the sled runners and cut the ropes holding the load on the sled.

She could hear him tell Quiet Rabbit to run. She listened as Taelo shouted out for everyone to lay their sleds down. Then he disappeared from sight as he and the sled went over the edge!

Feather-in-the-Wind took all the rope she had in her sled and ran toward Taelo. Just before the sled went down into the crevasse, she saw Taelo tie the anchor rope to the wolves pull harness. He would be on his head when the sled went over!

The rope tied to Taeko's spear was singing from the strain of the weight. Feather-in-the-Wind put her entire weight on the spear to drive it farther into the snow and ice and to prevent it from bending over. Miraculously the rope held.

She tied her rope to Taelo's spear and threw it over the edge of the crevasse.

She watched Burley Bear fling Quiet Rabbit back the entire length of his sled as he ran past her with a rope that he tossed over the edge. He then laid down and approached the edge of the crevasse. He was joined by Saber Scar.

She was between them and took a quick look over the edge. She immediately backed away as vertigo swept over her. She had seen Taelo still hanging onto the sled.

She had seen the sled, Taelo and the wolf team all hanging on the single line. Taelo was taking the time to tie the line she has thrown down to the sled and to the wolf harness line.

She stood up and backed away from the crevasse. She went back to get everything ready to pull the sled back up. She stopped to hug Quiet Rabbit and to let her know that Taelo was alright.

She then watched as, Saber Scar and Burley Bear each reached down and as if by magic they hoisted Taelo back onto the surface.

A feeling of relieve swept over her as she heard Taelo comment that getting pulled up felt like he was flying like a bird as he thanked both Burley Bear and Saber Scar.

She, Running Stag and Busy Bee had organized three teams to pull the sled back up.

"Saber Scar, Burley Bear, please join your teams," Busy Bee called out.

"I see that you have put the Others and Little Otter in the back as the anchors," Taelo commented to Busy Bee as Talking Wren called out the cadence.

"Yes, but the problem will be when the sled makes it to the top. We will need Burley Bear's and Saber Scar's combined strength to pull it up and over the edge.

Taelo ran to end of the pull line and asked Whistling Arrow and Little Otter to join him. He planted a spear as deep into the snow as possible. He then looped the line onto on spear at the surface of the snow. He had them do the same with two more spears and ran the same rope around their spears. They would be the anchor when Saber Scar and Burley Bear pulled the sled up out of the crevasse. Each time the sled moved up, they would pull the rope tight and lock it in place.

She listened as he then assigned Running Stag and White Bear to take two of the spots.

She watched as he went to where Burley Bear and Saber Scar were lifting the sled over the edge. He lent his strength to the final effort and the sled came up over the edge and fell on its runners.

The line to the wolves was still secure and holding. He and Whistling Arrow then began to pull the wolves up one at a time. When a wolf was near the top edge, Whistling Arrow would hold Taelo's legs as he slid forward, reached down with both arms, and lifted the wolf up over his shoulder.

The wolves immediately ran to her, and she gave each a hug and a treat. This cycle repeated until, finally Lasher was pulled back over the edge.

The sun had brushed the few clouds in the sky an orange and maroon mix of color. Out on the horizon an eagle let out a cry.

"I hope that is a cry of victory and not another cry of warning," Taelo called out as he looked up at the sky.

Feather-in-the-Wind got tears in her eyes as she overheard Quiet Rabbit thank Taelo for launching her back to Burley Bear's sled.

"Other than being bruised by having been thrown through the air twice I am just fine," Quiet Rabbit said as she sat next to Taelo as they both hugged and talked to the wolves.

"I can't tell you how my heart stopped when you went over the edge," Quiet Rabbit whispered quietly as she once again brushed her hand across the side of Taelo's face.

Feather-in-the-Wind had watched Burley Bear throw Quiet Rabbit back even farther. She had never seen Burley Bear move so fast.

She had wanted to join in on the pulling and lifting but instead she had stepped out of the way and organized the rest of the people.

Floating Cloud had arranged a small fire built on a flat stone held above the ice by two sticks with forked legs driven down into the snow. She made stew for Taelo and everyone that had helped in the rescue effort.

"I would like to cook for all of you but there is not enough wood. When I am done, I will have used all of the fish trap for fuel." Floating Cloud announced to those watching.

No one objected. They had all seen the effort that Taelo's team had exerted to save him. They were in awe of the reaction speed and seamless coordination the team had displayed.

One point of discussion was how easily both Taelo and Burley Bear had thrown Quiet Rabbit through the air.

"She is not that small. She is twice my size and Burley Bear threw her the length of his sled and wolf team. She must have bruises all over," Bubbling Brook commented.

"She may be bruised but she is safe," Bending Willow replied.

The next day, Feather-in-the-Wind watched as Taelo, and Golden Hawk took the lead. Lasher was their lead wolf.

When Lily's camp came into view, Feather-in-the-Wind heard Golden Hawk joke about how well he had done in keeping Taelo from falling into another crevasse.

"It seems the team here has made the cover larger. I wonder if they have any idea about the number of people we are bringing," Busy Bee observed.

"They are about to find out. I hope they have plenty of food because we are coming in empty handed. We lost half of our supplies when the sled went over the edge," Talking Wren commented.

"Let's hope the buffalo herd has its winter home in this area. Golden Hawk and Taelo will lead a hunting party to replenish our supplies," Quiet Rabbit added.

"Welcome back. Let me guide your sleds into position," Lily called out as she ran forward and gave Taelo a hug. Lily continued down the line giving greeting hugs.

"Oh, my, I will need to recruit some help to feed all of you," Lily said loudly as she guided Taelo's sled into position.

"It is good to see that everyone is coming back in good shape," Single Leaf greeted the team.

"Well, I think everyone is in good shape. I on the other hand was man handled by Taelo and Burley Bear and I am one big bruise," Quiet Rabbit gave a quiet reply to Single Leaf.

She then went on to briefly recall the incident out on the ice.

The White Bear Clan members entered the enclosure and were surprised at the size and the available space.

"So, my bruised Quiet Rabbit, do you approve of our area between the sleds," Taelo said as he stripped off his outer clothes.

"Lily, Single Leaf, Slow Runner and Sharp Blade have done an excellent job at being ready for us.

"What a wonderful lodge," Whistling Arrow commented as he walked around and noted its design.

"There is a space between each sled for the owners of the sleds to occupy. Please make your sleeping area out by each sled. There is enough room for everyone to have a comfortable sleeping area. The center of the lodge is for us to gather around the warming fire and converse," Lily said in the tongue of the White Bear Clan.

"How is it that so many speak our language," Bending Willow wondered out loud.

"I am Lily. Taelo rescued me and several others including Running Stag from the cannibals. I come from the other side of the ice bridge," Lily replied to the question.

"Where are the cannibals now," Whistling Arrow asked?

"There are none left on this side of the ice bridge.

Taelo, Quiet Rabbit, Busy Bee, Running Stag, Golden Hawk, Burley Bear, Saber Scar, and their warriors fought and killed them. My mate and I fought them also. I lost my mate and many of my friends," Bashful Lark replied.

This trip had been her closure journey. She had wanted to see the land she had left and to remember the journey she and her mate had made across the ice bridge in their attempt to escape the cannibals. Her heart still ached with the memory of her lost mate.

She and Whistling Arrow had a warm friendship and she hope this would lead to something more. She would wait and see what would happen at the meeting of the clan.

"We will need to increase our food reserve. Where is the buffalo herd," Golden Hawk asked as they sat around the central fire?

"The herd moves around the valley to the east. We will be able to hunt and get all the meat we need. Fishing is also very good so we should be able to setup the fish trap. We have enough hands so that we can catch and smoke many fish," Sharp Blade replied

"I will take a team out to the river to setup the fish trap in the morning," Single Leaf volunteered.

"Let my fishing team capture and process the fish," Whistling Arrow offered when he heard about the fishing.

"That would be great," was Single Leaf's reply.

For the next few sun cycles Feather-in-the-Wind joined Taelo and Golden Hawk as they studied Quiet Rabbit's and Busy Bee's drawings of their journey. The goal was to return and arrive in time for the Elk Clan's autumn gathering.

Taelo studied the way back. The buffalo outside of their camp was depicted in bright orange, the bear was represented in black, the gap through to the valley on the far side was in white, the long valley beyond in dark green.

Taelo, Golden Hawk and Feather-in-the-Wind discussed how to handle the giant bears. With so many people to take through, he felt they needed to do something different.

Each of Taelo's team had taken on some critical role and task that needed doing. They spent an evening sharing their progress.

"The language classes have been making great progress. By the time we get to the clan meeting everyone will know the Elk Clan tongue," Running Stag shared with the team.

"We have been processing the hides and have been making clothes for each White Bear Clan member and we have also been making many to trade during the coming clan meeting," Meadow Flower shared.

"We will have slings, arrows, spearheads, some stone axes, bone needles and many more items that we have been making," Feather-in-the-Wind said as she leaned against Running Stag.

"We are bringing many people back with us. We must present ourselves as successful, industrious people that will enhance the Elk Clan," Quiet Rabbit added.

"We have never been so busy and productive. We are very impressed with how you have improved the lives of the White Bear Clan," Deer Chaser interjected

"Yes, and we have learned an exciting way to hunt that we are looking forward in trying when we go out with Saber Scar to hunt the buffalo," White Bear said with enthusiasm.

"Splitting up and becoming members of the various Elk sub-clans is a point of concern for some of us," Bubbling Brook spoke up from behind Deer Chaser.

"This will be necessary. But we will make sure we match you with the sub-clan of your choice. For some of you it will also be a chance to find a mate.

Talk with Lily and Bashful Lark. They have each experienced this. Many of their friends are now in the various Elk sub-clans," Quite Rabbit replied.

"I just want all in the White Bear Clan to understand that our team is made up of members of three of the Elk Clan sub-clans. Some of us are from the Northern Elk Clan, some are from the Clan of the Others and I and Little Otter are from the original Elk Clan.

Taelo and Golden Hawk are Golden Feather warriors and belong to all the Clans," Talking Wren shared.

"I will tell you that the Elk Clan and all its sub-clans will allow you to find the home you desire. The fall gathering is always the highlight where old friends reconnect, love affairs begin and where most find their mates.

Some, like me, will find it more difficult to find another mate. You will notice though that I now have my handsome Slow Runner," Lily added as she pushed Slow Runner out in front of everyone.

"There are many concerns.

All of them will have a positive resolution. No one will be asked to do something they do not wish to do.

"It has been a grueling ten sun cycles. The White Bear Clan members are wondering if all this practice and preparation is necessary," Whistling Arrow said as he finished his evening dinner.

"You will know when we face the dangers for which we have been getting you ready," Burley Bear replied.

"We all have asked the same question in the past and each time the practice saved us," Little Otter added.

"We have no complaints. Deer Chaser and I have learned to hunt as Taelo and Golden Hawk hunt. We are constantly learning from Saber Scar and Sharp Blade, and we now feel confident to cook our own food after learning from Lily and Floating Cloud," White Bear said in defense.

"Thank you for speaking up. I will tell you from experience, each of us will need to contribute our part in making sure we protect each other.

We will practice for the entire trip back to the valley of the gathering," Talking Wren spoke up.

Taelo had been listening quietly. He felt much like the rest of the team members.

"I think it is time for us to begin our trip to the south," he quietly mentioned to Quiet Rabbit.

"I agree. It is time to act. We will break camp in four sun cycles and begin our journey back to the territories of the Elk Clan and the Others," Taelo announced.

"I will manage the preparation of the camp for our departure," Meadow Flower volunteered.

"Marigold and I will organize the packing of the sleds," Lily added.

"Running Stag and I will make sure we have the food for the wolves," Feather-in-the-Wind went on.

"Saber Scar and I will make sure all the sled travois and the harnesses for the mounts are in good shape," Slow Runner added his voice.

"Busy Bee and I will work with all the families to ensure each has enough food for the trip and is prepared to move their family," Quiet Rabbit went on.

"I will arrange for a traveling cooking crew that will make everyone the evening meal. Feather-in-the-Wind has continued training everyone on the use of the sling and has told them about hunting as we travel. If everyone does their part, we should be able to have a mix of fresh meat and stews made from the meat we have dried," Floating Cloud spoke up.

"Well, I sense a great pent up energy of anticipation. Thank you all for volunteering to handle a part of the load," Taelo said when it was clear everyone had expressed themselves.

Chapter 19:

Feather-in-the-Wind thought about the how the way back was really always a new way. The same distant white topped mountains, their skirts of dark green sentinel pine trees appearing to be close but almost as far away as the ancients, graced both sides of the path back home but it was a new way. The world now took on the backward look as left became right and right became left. The mind wanted order, it simplified the vision and accepted the difference.

She knew that up was still up and that right and left meant little.

She and Taelo had agreed on a new way to handle the giant bears. She reminded him of feeding the wolves and his previous encounters with bears and feeding them. The animals were seeking survival. They needed to eat. She suggested feeding the attacking bear. He had chuckled and thanked her for reminding him of what had been successful for him.

Taelo shared the plan that he, she, and Golden Hawk had in how to handle an attacking bear.

It was different than what they had done on the way up. They had learned from that experience and designed an approach that they thought better fit guiding such a large group through the bear's territory. The smell that such a large group would put into the air was bound to attract every bear for a great distance around.

"Taelo has faced many bears. His most successful encounter was when he fed the bear.

His next encounter with a huge bear that had chased me up a tree, almost cost him his life.

The first encounter on the way north almost cost me my life.

The second encounter went much better, and the bear also survived," Feather-in-the-Wind continued the explanation.

"Now on the way back we will be prepared to use everything we learned," she continued.

"We will have three travois loaded with good smelling meat. When the bear attacks, we will lure it away with the meat.

The rest of you will proceed at a full jog until one of us calls a halt. All of you have been trained in the use of the sling and each of you will carry a sack of sharp stone shards. Should we need to take a stand, we will take turns using our slings pelting the bear in the eyes. This should stun it long enough for everyone to turn and run.

Again, Taelo, Running Stag or I will leave a load of food near the bear," Golden Hawk added.

"We hope in this way to buy our way across the bear territory and keep the risk low to both the bear and to us,"

"I will organize slinger teams that will always come to the aid of any group facing a bear. Once this group gets into position, the group that was attacked will jog away and get back to their normal position," Feather-in-the-Wind shared with everyone listening.

"Burley Bear and I have been recruited to play the attacking bears. Please do not use your slings on us," Little Otter spoke up.

"I have assigned everyone a place in our caravan. You will maintain this order for the entire trip all the way to the valley where the Elk Clan holds its meeting," Talking Wren announced.

"It's no wonder this team defeated the Sky Eyes," Whistling Arrow commented to White Bear.

"I agree, if the bears want to live, they better follow the script," Deer Chaser added,

Two sun cycles later Feather-in-the-Wind praised everyone on their practice performance.

"The camp has been cleared and the area put back as close to what we found as possible. By next spring nature will have this area back to its original condition," Talking Wren reported to the rest of the team as they were about ready to leave.

"My slingers are ready. Quiet Rabbit is the leader of one team. Busy Bee has another team. Bashful Lark leads a third team and Floating Cloud leads a fourth team. These teams will be dispersed along the travel line and come together at the point of attack," Feather-in-the-Wind reported next.

"Taelo, Running Stag and I have our gift tied to a travois we are pulling with our mounts. As you all know we decided that we needed one gift in the front, one in the middle and one at the back of our long line. Thanks to Lily for preparing our pieces of meat," Golden Hawk announced.

The caravan began its journey. It was hard for those in the rear to see those in front. The wolves were pulling the sleds. The sleds ran in parallel pairs. The slingers were walking or jogging next to the sleds.

"We are well into the area and so far, we have only frightened a few rabbits and scared some geese," Taelo commented to Burley Bear.

"It's time to make camp. We will need to station ourselves around the camp. We will space offering and slingers around the rest of the group. I hope these animals don't hunt in the night," Burley Bear commented.

"Well, if they are anything like the bear in our area, they indeed do hunt at night especially when there is enough light like it is in this area," Golden Hawk replied when he heard what Burley Bear had said.

The eagle cry in the sky put everyone on alert.

"Let's move our meat offering out away from the clan. Put up small fires all around the edge of our camp. Quickly gather enough wood to keep the fires going all night. Put the slinger teams at each offering location but inside the fire ring," Taelo rattled off his instruction.

It was early next morning when there was a roar at the northern tail end of the camp.

Taelo, Golden Hawk and Running Stag ran to their meat offerings.

"I have him he is mine, Taelo called out as he quickly pulled the large chunk of meat toward the bear.

There had not been enough time to put the travois on his mount, so he took the meat and began to drag it away from the camp.

The slingers had done their work and stalled the bear. The smell of the meat did the trick, and the bear began to chase after Taelo. It was clear that the bear would quickly catch up to Taelo.

Suddenly another person began pulling the meat along with Taelo.

"I am not letting a giant bear catch you," Quiet Rabbit said as she ran alongside of Taelo putting her strength into the pull.

"And I certainly don't want him to have you either," Taelo shouted as he accelerated with all his might.

The bear was slowly gaining. The camp was now out of sight.

"Ok let go and run with me," Taelo instructed.

An eagle scream came from somewhere ahead.

"Did you see the bravery of those two? Quiet Rabbit turned her concern for Taelo into an action of pure bravery," Bashful Lark commented to Long Leaper.

Not long after, Feather-in-the-Wind saw Taelo and Quiet Rabbit return.

Busy Bee was riding up front pulling the next offering of meat.

Quiet Rabbit went to her position with her slinger team and Taelo ran up to where Busy Bee was and reclaimed his mount.

"Thank you for filling in for me. I am sure the bear would much prefer to be served by you," Taelo joked with Busy Bee.

"You're welcome and I am pleased to give up this honor," Busy Bee said as she dropped down and let the procession pass her by until she was with her team of slingers.

"See how naturally the team adjusts at the critical moments. The action taken by Quiet Rabbit helping Taelo and Busy Bee taking up Taelo's position were not planned action but because they had the rest of us doing what was required of us, they were able to make quick adjustments that seemed seamless and planned.

We can learn so much by just watching and learning from them," Whistling Arrow commented to White Bear.

"I have learned as much in the last few moons as all the time before," White Bear replied.

The next attack came two sun cycles later. The bear attacked the side of the column guarded by Floating Cloud and her team of slingers.

Floating Cloud let out the attack cry the team had practiced and let her shards of stone fly from her sling.

"Sling slingers sling," everyone heard her cry.

Running Stag reacted immediately and guided his mount between the slingers and the bear. He paused long enough for the bear to get the scent of the offered meat and then when the bear started to follow, Running Stag turned his mount and led the bear away from the caravan.

"It seems to be working. Let's keep the caravan moving. Its double pace for the next few cycles" Burley Bear called back to everyone.

"Running Stag has slowed his mount to let the bear keep up easily. He is slowly taking the bear farther out. He has now dropped the meat and he has stopped a short distance away. The bear is now fully engaged in eating. Running Stag is now moving away at a rapid pace," Feather-in-the-Wind announced from where she stood on her moving mount.

There is always a surprise with this team. Feather-in-the-Wind is standing on her mount as it continues moving with the column. Her entire attention is in watching what Running Stag is doing," Whistling Arrow commented.

"I know that she helped Taelo kill one of these bears on their journey up through this area. She has a long scar on her thigh from such a bear. She is known for her bravery.

She was also key in killing a giant tiger on their last journey," White Bear replied.

"Where did you learn all this," Whistling Arrow asked?

"I have learned to watch and listen," White Bear said with a smile.

"That is quite a change from one who normally likes to talk and talk," Deer Chaser teased.

"Both of us have grown and our recent experience has changed us. Thanks to Taelo and his team our entire clan has survived a terrible ordeal and we seem to be on a path to a better life," Deer Chaser commented.

"The meat is a small price to pay. Keeping this many people safe as we travel is a major challenge. The weather is not done with us. We will want to be through the gap before the spring thaw floods the narrow channel," Taelo commented over the end of day meal.

"High waters will indeed make it much more difficult even though we will be going with the river this time," Burley Bear added.

The streams from the north joined together and soon the river, that flowed through the gorge and that mirrored its path with the blue of the sky, formed. As the bear country seemed to come to an end, the river seemed to become gentler and flowed more easily.

The days though still cold gave way to the warmth of the sun. The fish trap kept the entire group well fed and the small army of slingers bagged an amount of small game that allowed everyone a selection they had rarely enjoyed.

The day came when the snow gave way to grass, and the sleds had to be put on the travois poles and be pulled by the mounts.

As the White Bear Clan watched the transition from sleds on the ground to sleds on the travois, they were again impressed with the genius of the team that had rescued them.

Now all goods were being pulled on travois. Every mount and two dozen people were pulling the goods needed to sustain over one hundred people.

Two moon cycles later the river arrived at the gap. The water was higher than before but not yet at the flood level that the spring thaw would bring.

"How will we get through this gap? Is there another way around," Whistling Arrow asked as he stood looking at what looked like and impassable point in their journey?

"Our raft is up along the base of the cliff. We will be able to float all our goods and wolves through. We will want many of you to cross on a narrow ledge along the cliff. Those who we think are too young or may have problems with the narrow ledge will be floated down with the goods," Golden Hawk replied.

"I will organize the transit," Talking Wren commented as she entered into the conversation.

"We will setup camp on this side and plan on several sun cycles for the transit," Taelo continued.

"Talking Wren and I have agreed that Busy Bee and I will establish a second camp on the other side of the Gap in the location we used on our way up. This will let us make the transit in as many sun cycles as we need. There is not a rush other than getting through before the spring flood," Quiet Rabbit added.

"Once again this round robin of leadership amazes me," Whistling Arrow thought to himself.

It was clear to him that those around Taelo flowed naturally to do what needed to be done. They did not even seem to realize how different they were and how smooth their daily interactions were.

"Leaders normally struggle with each other to control the situation in a manner they desire. Taelo seems to encourage a flow of differing ideas and causes the team to converge in what seems a natural flow.

However, if you listen closely you will always hear him asking the questions that bring the team to a common conclusion," Whistling Arrow shared with Dear Chaser and White Bear.

"Now that you mentioned this, it is obvious to me," Dear Chaser replied.

"I hope to learn how to do this," White Bear added as he thought how effective and efficiently Taelo's team operated.

The upstream camp was setup without the central cover. The cover, and the poles would be floated through the gap first. This would allow the second camp to be established before sending the White Bear Clan's younger children and the large amount of goods that needed to be sheltered.

The raft was assembled. The platform with the woven floor was mounted across the two bundles of logs on which everything floated. The first load took the cover and most of the stronger young men who would follow Marigolds and Saber Scars instruction and setup the lodge.

A mix of wolves and the younger children were the next to go through the gap.

The mounts provided the power in pulling and letting the rafts move down stream. Even then the work of loading and unloading the raft was a strain on everyone.

Taelo and Talking Wren continually adjusted what was on the raft. They had a plan, but they were opportunistic and made sure the raft was loaded fully for each trip.

After two sun cycles the sleds were sent through the gap and then it was time to change the configuration of the raft and take the mounts through.

Bashful Lark suggested they keep the mounts out of the water by strapping them in on the beams that made up the platform. This would keep their bodies out of the cold water.

A pull line attached to the raft could be floated downstream.

The raft would be pulled up on the beach, the mounts strapped in. Then the upstream team could push the raft, while the downstream pulled the raft until it was back in the water.

At this point the upstream members could feed the line and let the current pull the raft through the gap.

"Let's give this idea a try. We have enough pullers downstream and if we are successful, our mounts will not experience the freeze they did before," Taelo enthusiastically said in support.

The approach accelerated the transfer of the mounts and within two more sun cycles they were all through

Burley Bear, Meadow Flower, Saber Scar, Marigold, Sharp Knife, Single Leaf, Little Otter, Golden Hawk, and Taelo were the members of the team that guided the last mount through the gap and then pulled the raft back up to the beach for the last time.

"This has been plain hard work," Burley Bear commented as they pulled the raft up stream.

"Yes, it has been hard. The camp at the other side is now fully operational. Tonight, we will all be sleeping in the comfort of our lodge.

Floating Cloud and Lily are preparing a special dinner for all of you.

They have the red fish ready to roast and they sent Feather-in-the-Wind and Running Stag and a few others out to hunt for a boar or some other game as well.

The dried food we left here is exactly what we needed but we will need to hunt and get more," Talking Wren shared.

Taelo had enrolled several of the White Bear Clan to help in handling the last load and had listened to their banter. White Bear and Dear Chaser were two of the most vocal.

"I agree we struggled to control letting the raft go down stream. All of us together would not be able to pull it back upstream," Dear Chaser commented.

"This young man is just trying to get on our good side," Marigold teased as she pulled to the cadence Meadow Flower was calling out.

"If he wants to be on my good side, he will come over here and take my place," Single Leaf grunted as she pulled.

"This is our last pull," Meadow Flower commented as the empty raft came back upstream.

"I am amazed that everything went so smoothly," Talking Wren commented.

Taelo was very aware to the fact that the power of the Others was one of the reasons the transit had gone so well.

He had tried to relieve them as much as possible but as always, the strength of the Others was once again the main reason for the team's success.

"We will put the raft up as high as possible along the cliff. Perhaps someday someone will find use for it again," Burley Bear said as the team pulled the raft up on the beach.

"It does seem like a waste for it not to be used again," Taelo commented.

"We need to take care getting across the gap. I will cross first. Each of you keep watch on the person in front of you. It is not hard just a little tricky," Talking Wren said as she went across the gap.

"I will come across with Burley Bear and the pull team," Taelo said as he realized Talking Wren was crossing over.

"Let's all take a rest before we cross on the ledge," Meadow Flower suggested.

"I agree. My arm muscles are a little shaky," Little Otter replied.

"I think Talking Wren forgot that she asked me to bring over a bag of our honey drink for all of you.

She has gone ahead because the team has a special meal, they are preparing for you," Taelo said as he handed the bag to Burley Bear.

"Very nice," Burley Bear commented as he took a sip and then passed the bag to Meadow Flower.

By the time the bag went all the way around and came back to Taelo it was empty.

High in the sky an eagle let out a cry.

"I think it just told me I should have had my share before passing the bag to Burley Bear," Taelo joked.

He hoped that the cry was just that and not a warning about a new danger.

Feather-in-the-Wind asked what the cry of the eagle at this time meant.

"I am not sure, but I am going to the river to look around. Want to come with me," Quiet Rabbit replied.

"Running Stag and I are going to scout the area to the south," Feather-in-the-Wind replied as she went to the river.

"What should the rest of us do, Deer Chaser asked?

"Just tell everyone to be alert and ready for whatever action we need to take," Talking Wren replied.

"I am going up to the crossing," she continued.

Burly Bear was in the lead as the team made its way along the ledge. Everyone was concentrating on getting across.

"I feel so out of shape," Little Otter commented when he slipped and almost fell.

"Steady, there are only a few more spear lengths," Saber Scar said as he steadied Little Otter.

Taelo took one last look behind him. The beach was empty. The pieces of raft were neatly stacked up against the cliff. The area was clean and restored to its original tranquil condition.

He would always remember the first night he had spent there with Quiet Rabbit as they were heading to the North. The multiple points of light and the play of the web of different colored lights glowing across above them had touched them both as they lay comfortably and fell asleep. The rising sun had accented the immeasurable height of the cut through which the river flowed. This would be a lifelong memory.

He turned and followed Single Leaf along the ledge.

"I am feeling a little dizzy," Single Leaf said quietly.

Then she moaned and seemed to let go and fall slowly backwards into the swiftly moving water shooting through the gap.

The water was ice cold, and it was crystal clear. Taelo saw Single Leaf submerged a short distance from where she had entered the water. Her foot was wedged between two boulders. He jumped in and then flipped around to go down stream feet first. He got his feet planted firmly one on each boulder. The force of the water caused him to use all his strength to maintain his position. He could see the fear in Single Leaf's eyes as he reached down to pull her foot out from where it was trapped.

When her foot came free the two shot rapidly down the stream like a swiftly flying spear.

He pulled what seemed like a lifeless body from the water and carried her hanging from his shoulder in the way he remembered Grey Weaver telling him it should be done.

His legs almost buckled under her weight. He bounced Single Leaf on his shoulder. He would have to tell Grey Weaver how hard it was to lift one of the Others to one's shoulder. He saw water drain from her mouth. It was happening just as Grey Weaver had told him.

He put Single leaf down and blew air into her.

"Speak to me," Taelo said as he realized how cold he was.

"I am very cold. Are we alive or is this the next world," Single Leaf said a few moments later in her own tongue?

As cold and miserable as I feel at the moment. I hope we are alive. I want the next world to be warm and gentle," Taelo replied.

Taelo saw the entire team rushing downstream toward the two of them.

"We will soon be warm and well fed. Let's see if we can stand and help each other walk back up the river. I am sure Sharp Blade will be helping you in the next few minutes," Taelo said as he helped Single Leaf stand up.

"I have never seen anything like this. We could see down into the water from above. Single Leaf let out a groan. Fell into the water and sank like a stone. The water wedged her against two boulders. We all knew it was too late for Single Leaf. She let out the last of her air and went limp. We thought we had lost them both until we heard Quiet Rabbit shout and point downstream," Burley Bear began the story.

"I saw Taelo jump in after Single Leaf and was sure it was the end," Talking Wren took over.

"When Quiet Rabbit pointed Taelo out, he had picked up Single Leaf on his shoulder and was bouncing her up and down. Then he laid her flat on the ground and breathed into her and then pressed on her chest. He did this several times until Single Leaf began to cough and then sat up looking around.

"We all let out a cheer as we ran toward them.

Sharp Blade outran all of us. We now know what can make him run as fast as any of us," Talking Wren finished.

"I must thank Taelo for saving my life. I think I saw the light of the land of the ancestors but then I heard Taelo talking to me telling me it was not yet my time. Now, I owe him a debt and must ask how to repay it," Single Leaf commented as she sat and let the fire warm her.

"In life we learn many things even when we think we are just listening to stories. I listened to the stories told by my father and later found them to be the true stories of our ancestors. I listened to the stories of Grey Weaver and learned many things that I have used. He talked of feeding the wolves and the bears as a way to control them. I did this first on the beach where we found the whale. We used this approach on our way through the giant bear country and it worked better than battling the bear.

He also told me how to save someone who had drowned. He told Golden Hawk and me how to take the water out of the body of the person that was drowned and then how to blow new air into them.

So, your debt is not to me but to an old warrior named Grey Weaver. At the coming clan meeting, you will repay the debt. You and I will tell this story to the entire clan and praise his teachings. Then we will serve him the best meal we know how to prepare.

Finally, on each anniversary of this day until he goes to his ancestors you and I will visit with him," Taelo replied. "I owe him as much as you do."

"It is no wonder that all of you follow Taelo anywhere he wishes to go," Whistling Arrow commented to Bashful Lark.

"Yes, and I now understand my total dedication to my granddaughter's mate," Floating Cloud, thought to herself, as she dried the tears from her eyes.

It amazed her how much comfort she found in being around Taelo's team.

Chapter 20:

Feather-in-the-Wind rode lazily enjoying the weather. She figured that sunshine and calm after a storm was preferable to the calm before the storm. The late summer journey toward the southeast through terrain with an abundant mix of small game, buffalo and elk allowed the team and the people they were leading to stock up on food.

A treasure was found as she and Saber Scar crested the hill and spotted a herd of mounts. This was an opportunity that could not be passed up. The team stopped to organize the capture of additional mounts.

The team discussed how to capture the mounts out on the open plain.

"Why not use you fish trap idea, we could use all our members as the guides into a pen or trap," Bashful Lark suggested.

The idea was immediately taken on.

Running Stag found a suitable small cliff lined valley with an opening into the valley where the mounts were grazing.

Everyone was given a long stick with a piece of leather on it. They were assigned a location out on the plain. Together they formed a slowly converging cone that would guide the mounts into the small holding valley.

Taelo, Golden Hawk, Quiet Rabbit, Busy Bee, Feather-in-the-Wind, Running Stag and Talking Wren were the riders guiding the mounts into the opening of the cone. They slowly moved the herd they had gathered into the cone. They moved slowly to keep the herd from bolting in alarm.

The line of people slowly waved their leather topped poles back and forth. As planned the herd went into the valley.

Burley Bear and his team closed the valley off once the last of the mounts trotted in.

There were enough mounts that every member of the White Bear Clan would have one mount.

Taelo and his team would have three each.

"Let's plan on traveling directly to the valley of the clan meeting. If we arrive early, we can spend time arranging for everyone's arrival. In the past we have been successful with the approach of feeding everyone and getting on their good side. We are bringing in enough people to make another clan and we bring enough mounts that these new members will be in good standing. They will all be well to do members.

How do we want to handle this," Taelo put the question to the team?

"I come from the far southern mountains where supposedly the great Condor has taken me for his bride. I came North with Taelo's team, and I made the *Journey of Discovery* to the East, and I swam the sea on that far side. I have now traveled North and survived the Great Bear and the Sky Eyes. North, South, West, East, we live in a giant land with giant beasts and many challenges. I would like to take a clan to the East and establish a home in the bay where Taelo saved Golden Hawk from the giant shark. Just to the south is the singing beach. I remember walking there and the laughter that graced my throat," Feather-in-the-Wind spoke up.

She had shared this vision with Running Stag and was now putting her desire out in front of the rest of the team.

"This will be a great challenge to the Elk Clan leadership. I know of four leaders that will support such a vision. I wonder if we will have enough family members willing to travel so far away," Quiet Rabbit responded as she absorbed what Feather-in-the-Wind was proposing.

"I know every family coming from the White Bear Clan would be willing to be led by Feather-in-the-Wind," Whistling Arrow commented in support.

It was a new concept for him, but he realized that Feather-in-the-Wind was a true leader and what he said reflected what other members of the White Bear Clan believed.

"You have my support. I can think of no one better to establish the Eastern Elk Clan," Taelo answered in support.

"The legend of Feather-in-the-Wind is now beginning," Golden Hawk added as he crossed over and gave her a hug.

"I will work with Talking Wren and Quiet Rabbit to devise a way to create the situation where we will win the needed support," Busy Bee said.

"We will also need to think about how to integrate our new members across all the clans. Once again, we arrive with more women than men and need to see about getting them mates," Talking Wren continued the conversation.

"We will need to get word to Feather-in-the-Wind's family," Taelo commented to Golden Hawk as the two rode their mounts out ahead of the procession following them.

"Well, I don't know of anyone available to send other than you and I. Everyone else will be engaged in running the clans. Do you think Quiet Rabbit and Busy Bee are up to a quick trip south," Golden Hawk replied?

"Well let's first get through the clan meeting. Then we can bring up the subject of a quick trip south.

The trip to the meeting valley took on the flavor of a traveling school.

246

Feather-in-the-Wind continued teaching anyone interested the use of the sling. She had all the younger members of the White Bear Clan in her following.

She was an adored person.

Her top student was Single Leaf who soon was as good and whose throwing range was at least fifty percent greater. A young boar made the mistake of running across in front of the caravan.

Single Leaf ran forward with her sling in full motion and hit the boar from at least ten mount lengths away. She continued running and as the boar struggled to get up, she finished it with her war hammer.

She was beaming as she carried the boar back to her sled. She cleaned the boar as the caravan continued.

"Come to my campfire this evening," she invited the team members.

Later when the travois were circled and the camp setup the team gathered at Single Leaf's fire circle.

"Each of you has a boulder to sit on," Sharp Blade commented as he showed each member where to sit.

"The boar smells delicious," Quiet Rabbit commented as she took her seat.

"Today I saw my best sling student become a master. I must now claim to be almost as good as Single Leaf," Feather-in-the-Wind commented in praise.

"Perhaps you should wait a bit longer. I may just have been lucky," a beaming Single Leaf replied as she and Sharp Blade lifted the boar from the hot coals.

"This is the first chance that I have had to feed the person who saved me," Single Leaf commented as she cut the hind leg of the boar and handed it to Taelo.

"Thank you, this is much more than I can possibly eat by myself. Busy Bee, Golden Hawk please join us," Taelo commented as he accepted the leg and put it on the boulder in front of him.

"Your display with the sling surprised us all. I have never seen such accuracy at such a distance. We will keep this in mind for future encounters," Burley Bear added as he was given the other hind leg.

"Hey, is there going to be enough boar for all of us," Little Otter blurted out as Saber Scar was given a front leg.

"You should not worry so much. I am saving the tail for you," Single Leaf joked as she gave Talking Wren the other front Leg.

"To my sling teacher I present the head and the rest of us will eat from the side and back. Floating Cloud has promised that anyone still hungry is welcome to some rabbit, groundhog, or the pheasant she bagged today," Single Leaf said as she pointed to each offering.

Feather-in-the-Wind enjoyed the savory flavor of the meat as she looked around. Running Stag sat next to her and everyone around the fire had a mate sitting next to them. She felt the harmony and warmth in the friendship surrounding her.

"We will arrive early and will establish ourselves on the far side of the lake.

We will greet each sub-clan and help them setup camp. We have been successful at this once before. This time it will be easier, but we will want to flaunt our good standing and the industrious nature of our new members," Busy Bee commented as the team sat around the evening fire.

"Do you expect problems at the meeting because of us," Whistling Arrow inquired?

"No, the clan now expects a surprise from us every time we return from one of our journeys. It began when Grey Fox Running was promoted leader of the original Elk Clan.

"Is Taelo responsible for improving the role of women in the leadership of the clan," Whistling Arrow continued with a question that had been on his mind?

"No, that came from the Clan of the Others. Their women have always fought besides them and have been part of the Other's Clan of Elders.

Taelo learned that from them and with White Swan convinced the Elk Clan to allow women to hunt with him.

"I will say that the participation of women in leadership roles is the part that the men in the White Bear Clan have talked about the most. I suppose that this is also true of all the women. Your team's behavior has inspired all of us," Whistling Arrow replied.

Feather in the Wind sat quietly as the sun set on the far horizon. This was a horizon toward where she and the team were headed.

It would soon be the time for the clan meeting.

The team moved on and then a large herd of grazing buffalo along with a few elk seemed to present themselves. This was an opportunity for them to supply the clan meeting with fresh meat and hides.

Feather in the Wind knew that this would put everyone in a good position.

Golden Hawk proposed that she and Running Stag lead the caravan to the Elk Clan meeting valley.

The hunters would send the meat directly to the valley.

"Who will be allowed to stay and hunt," Bubbling Brook asked?

"Let's see if we can make this easy. Those who wish to stay and hunt step behind Burley Bear. Those who wish to go to the meeting valley step behind Feather-in-the-Wind," Quiet Rabbit suggested.

"Well, my friend, you seem to be more popular than Feather-in-the-Wind," Taelo said quietly to Burley Bear as two thirds of the caravan members got behind Burley Bear.

"It is clear that we have some young members who wish to be hunters. We are pleased with your desire but this time we will ask you to go with Feather-in-the-Wind," Busy Bee commented as she, Quiet Rabbit and Talking Wren sent each youngster to the other side.

The mothers of the youngsters went with them as well and in the end the split slightly favored Feather in the Wind.

Returning to a former place awakens the memories of the past. Good and bad memories are equally freed. The Elk Clan's meeting valley held very good memories for most of members of the expanded Elk Clan.

The mountain's dark green pine covered base sported many year-round white caps. These mountains surrounded the long peaceful now tan and gold covered grass covered valley. The long oblong lake fed by a bubbling stream running down from the far mountains and then leaving the valley in a quite stream was surrounded by the now yellowing cattails with their dark brown sausage tops and the weeping willows bending out over them was nestled at one end.

This was the site of the autumn meeting of the clan. This was the place many love affairs had taken root. This was the place the clan re-united their common purpose and adjusted the balance of the Elk Clan.

"It has been an interesting and exciting journey, but it will be a pleasure to see our friends and families," Busy Bee replied.

"I agree, though I really do not look forward to returning to my Valley of Plenty," Talking Wren added as she leaned forward viewing the valley.

The entire procession had stopped and were all gazing down into the valley.

"What a grand view," Long Leaper commented to Bashful Lark.

"This is only my second time, and it feels more like home than anywhere else I have lived," Bashful Lark commented.

"I understand your feelings. The Elk Clan has become my clan and I am more attached to those around me at the moment than my dear family far to the south," Feather-in-the-Wind added.

"Let's get down there and get setup on the other side of the lake before some other clan comes in ahead of us," Running Stag said as he urged his mount forward.

Feather in the Wind listened as Busy Bee, Floating Cloud and Quiet Rabbit conversed.

"Well, I see that you were able to get our detailed organizer to the other side of the lake so we could finish up in peace on this side," Busy Bee commented.

"She is great at getting things organized but once that is done, she begins to focus on details that drive me crazy," Floating Cloud replied.

"You should listen to her when she is discussing ideas for how to fight battles with Taelo and Golden Hawk. They listen intently and seldom argue with her. She has a keen mind. Taelo makes it a point of reviewing all her suggestions. He credits her with the idea for the shards to the eyes as a plan against a superior force," Quiet Rabbit commented.

"I can see her helping devise battle plans," Floating Cloud continued.

Talking Wren shared a layout for the campsites. Normally the first arrivals to the lake would randomly setup their camp. This random arrangement usually ended up with the camps of the last arrivals being very far from the lake. Her layout gave every sub-clan almost equal access to the lake no matter their arrival time.

While the White Bear Clan settled in on the far side of the lake, Talking Wren and a small team of helpers proceeded to lay out the side of the lake where the Elk Clans would have their camps.

Feather in the Wind knew that family gatherings always entertained and usually allowed everyone to catch-up on the latest accomplishments or issues their family and friends had faced. The coming together of the nine Elk Clans was like a large family get together. It had its moments of fun, its anxious moments, its feuding moments, and the serious moments when the leadership gathered to discuss the functioning and wellbeing of each clan.

For the last few seasons, Taelo and his team had made a significant impact. Even when he missed attending during two of the previous seasons, Taelo had been the center of attention.

Now Taelo and his team had once again come back with the equivalent of another sub-clan.

This would make the ninth Elk sub-clans and a total of ten clans counting the original Elk Clan.

What territory the new Elk Clan would get would be a hot topic of discussion and speculation.

The other sub-clans began to arrive. Talking Wren and her crew went out to help them take a place on the lake.

Busy Bee and Quiet Rabbit immediately visited each of the sub-clans and discussed the available young single women and men of the White Bear Clan.

"As in the past we are also looking to place families is each of the sub-clans. Please come to any of our evening meal gatherings for a wonderful feast and to meet these fine young people," Busy Bee said as she made her pitch once again.

The number of visitors to the evening meals grew significantly when word got out about the great food as well as the unattached young women and men.

"Once again you lead with the food and you succeed in your endeavor," Wise Owl said as he took part in his first evening meal.

"We have an over-abundance of young, single members. This clan lost most of their older leaders. Taelo has mentioned the desire to create the Eastern Elk Clan. To do this we will want to exchange families. The decision to establish another sub-clan needs to be one of the early decisions by the Leadership Council," Quiet Rabbit commented during her interaction with Wise Owl.

"Tomorrow late in the day will be the first meeting of the council. I will make sure this request is discussed. Are you supportive of Taelo's request as to the leader of this new sub-clan," Wise Owl inquired?

"Yes, all the people on this side of the lake are aware and supportive. This is what makes the family exchange so difficult. They all love the candidate Taelo has recommended and all wish to stay," Quiet Rabbit replied.

On the following day Wise Owl looked around the new council meeting area and then called the meeting to order.

He had asked Feather-in-the-Wind to sit outside.

"It is good that all the clans are having a good season," Wise Owl commented after the last clan gave its account of their preparedness for the coming winter.

"Taelo and Golden Hawk have returned from their journey to the North. They have brought us another clan worth of people and they have suggested we create another sub-clan to be called the Eastern Elk Clan. I support the establishment of this clan. Let me hear the discussion," Wise Owl announced.

"You all look to Taelo and then you look at me. This is the first I know of this suggestion. It seems to me a wise one as long as the Eastern Elk Clan settles beyond the territory of the Grazing Elk Clan," White Swan said in support.

"I too support the idea. It would be good to have a close neighbor." Fierce Badger the Grazing Elk Clan leader responded.

"Well, since I am supportive and I can count six of the nine clans are supportive as well, perhaps the other three will make this a unanimous decision. Who will lead this new sub-clan," Sleek Beaver of the Elk Hide Clan asked as he looked expectantly at Taelo?

"The leader I am recommending has been with me on three journeys. This person is a fearless warrior who has repeatedly demonstrated unparalleled courage, the ability to lead others and who has a commanding vision of the future.

She saved my life as together we defeated the great northern bear. I am recommending our Princess from the South, Feather-in-the-Wind be named leader of the Eastern Elk Clan and that Running Stag be named lead hunter," Taelo said as he slowly turned to make eye contact with each of the leaders around the circle.

He knew that naming a second woman as a leader would stretch the limit of the council's good will. Prior to the meeting, he, Quiet Rabbit, Golden Hawk and Busy Bee had visited each of the clan leaders and presented them with two mounts.

"Please, let's discuss this in an orderly manner," Wise Owl stepped into the center and took the meeting over as the surprised leaders were talking and shouting across to each other.

"Women are weak, women should tend to the fire, they should cure the hides and mind the children," Red Oak, now leader of the original Elk Clan stood up and slowly recited many of the lines he had often heard.

"What is all the fuss about? Have you examined the riches of the Northern Elk Clan? None of us can match their wealth. They have furs, tusks, shark's teeth, and an abundance of food. It must just be luck because they are led by a woman," Red Oak continued.

"Do you like the new layout of our meeting valley? It must be luck because a team of women planned the layout.

Did you like the food? Well, just as many of the young men cooked as did the young women.

It is time we quit basing our initial decision on gender and focus on the capability required for success.

Taelo has put forward a candidate and I suggest we take a vote," Red Oak said as he sat down.

"We will vote in two parts. First, we will vote on whether to setup a new clan and then we will vote on the leader," Wise Owl announced.

The vote to setup a new clan was unanimous.

The vote on the leader was six for and three against.

"Please call Feather-in-the-Wind into the meeting," Wise Owl requested of those at the edge of the meeting enclosure.

Feather-in-the-Wind came back from her remembrances that she had let play out in her mind and was now in the present moment. Her thoughts of the past had warmed her. Having Running Stag sit quietly beside her had calmed her.

Taelo and Golden Hawk came out and together they escorted Feather-in-the-Wind into the center of the leader's circle.

"Welcome to the leader's circle.

You have been selected to lead the Eastern Elk Clan.

Taelo says that the wolf has selected you as the eagle selected him. Your leader's spear has two wolves carved into it by Taelo and Golden Hawk

There is a blade carved by Saber Scar that represents the knife, your knife with which he killed the tiger.

There is a sling carved by Quiet Rabbit and Busy Bee.

The spear blade is a giant sharks tooth gifted by Burley Bear and the feather is of the giant Condor," Wise Owl pointed out each attribute as he presented the spear to a surprised Feather-in-the-Wind.

There were tears in her eyes as she ran her slender hand across the carvings made in her leader's spear.

She knew that Taelo and the rest of the team had called in all their favors to make it happen.

"I am humbled by this privilege.

The teachings of my father and mother will be my foundation.

The support of my close friends will be my sustenance.

The guidance of this wise council will be very important to me.

All the members of the Elk Clan, my clan, are always welcome at my fire ring," Feather-in-the-Wind said slowly and clearly as she looked at each of the other leaders in their eyes.

"This was my destiny to be with dear friends, my new family.

I wish my father and mother could know my happiness," Feather-in-the-Wind thought to herself as she took her seat in the ring of clan leaders.

Feather-in-the-Wind lay awake for the rest of the night. The rising sun found her walking along the edge of the lake pondering how to get more families to come over to the Eastern Elk Clan.

She approached Taelo and asked him to consider escorting her clan to their new home.

"Are you asking because of the difficulty of getting other Elk Clan families to join the Eastern Elk Clan," Taelo inquired?

"Yes, if you are a part of this then we will not have any problems getting the families to join," Feather-in-the-Wind replied truthfully.

She would have felt better to do this on her own, but she had to consider the members of her new clan.

"Then I suggest a two-step move. Your first step will be to move to our Paradise Valley for the winter. Our team will go with you there and help setup the camp for winter.

The ancestors have talked to me. There is a journey to the South that we must make. The Condor Clan needs our help.

This will give us an opportunity to let your family know that their princess has become a queen," Taelo replied and got the surprised look he expected from Feather-in-the-Wind.

"You are going to the land of the Condor! I wish I could go with you, but I know I could not even if I did not have the responsibility of the Eastern Elk Clan.

Who will be going with you," Feather-in-the-Wind inquired?

"We would love everyone to go with us but Golden Hawk, Quiet Rabbit, Busy Bee and I have discussed this at length. We extended our invitation to Saber Scar, Marigold, Single Leaf, Sharp Blade, White Bear and Deer Chaser. Our two camp managers Lily and White Cloud and their mates will join us as well," Taelo replied. Burley Bear like you would have loved to come but he too has a clan that he must lead.

Feather-in-the-Wind bowed her head and reached over and took Running Stag's hand. Her goal had been achieved. She had arrived to and was now looking into a rich and challenging future. She knew she would forever treasure the time she had spent learning and growing in the presence of those around her. She was with true friends.

She was where her dreams had come true. She was with the person that was her soul mate.

She was where she wanted to be.

The End

Thank You for reading this story.

Ron Mueller

<u>About the Author</u>
Ronald E. Mueller
remwriter95@gmail.com

Ron grew up in what is now Flint River State Park in Southeast Iowa. The 170-year-old house Ron lived in is built into a hillside. It faces a 125-foot high cliff towering over the little Flint River. The house and the land talked to him about the passing of time, the struggle to conquer the land, the struggles people faced and the wonder of nature.

He climbed the cliffs, crawled into the caves, dove from the swimming rock, collected clams from the bottom of the pond, gigged and skinned frogs for their legs. He trapped muskrats for fur, hunted raccoon in the dead of night, and hunted rabbits in the dead of winter with only a stick. His young life was outdoors, and nature tested him. He walked to a one-room, stone schoolhouse, uphill both ways. It was a great way to grow up.

His experiences inter-twined with snippets of fantasy lend themselves to the adventures Taelo leads the reader through.

Ron has told many similar stories to impart life values and influence the thinking of his children and now grandchildren. He feels stories are a wonderful means for parents and their children to engage in meaningful discussions about behavior and fundamental values and principles.

Books and Stories by Around the World Publishing

The Taelo Series by Ron Mueller
>   *Taelo: The Early Years*
>   *Taelo: The Golden Feather*
>   *Taelo: The Journey East*
>   *Taelo: Dangerous Passage*
>   *Taelo: Condor Clan Slingers*
>   *Taelo: Full Circle*

A Taelo Story:
>   The Name of the Child
>   White Swan and Quiet Pheasant
>   Broken Spear
>   Floating Cloud
>   Quiet Rabbit
>   Busy Bee
>   Little Otter& Talking Wren
>   Burley Bear & Meadow Flower

Science Fiction Books by Ron Mueller
>   The Door Series:
>   *The Door*
>   *Delivery*
>   *Journey Beyond*

>   The Savitar Series:
>   *Journey's End*
>   *Savitar*
>   *Confluence*

Single Science Fiction Books by Ron Mueller
>   *Current Past and Future*
>   *The Door*
>   *The Fold*

Books and Stories by Around the World Publishing

Fiction Books by Ron Mueller
    Event Survivors
The Problem Solver Series
    The Early Years
    Drug Lords
    Border Crossers

The Alex Evercrest Series
    The River Front
    The Girl on the Grill
    Missing
    Maggot

Imagination by Courtney Huynh and Chloe Parker

Around the World Publishing, LLC

QR Links to
ATWP.US web site

www.ingramcontent.com/pod-product-compliance
Lightning Source LLC
Chambersburg PA
CBHW070518100726
47907CB00004B/883